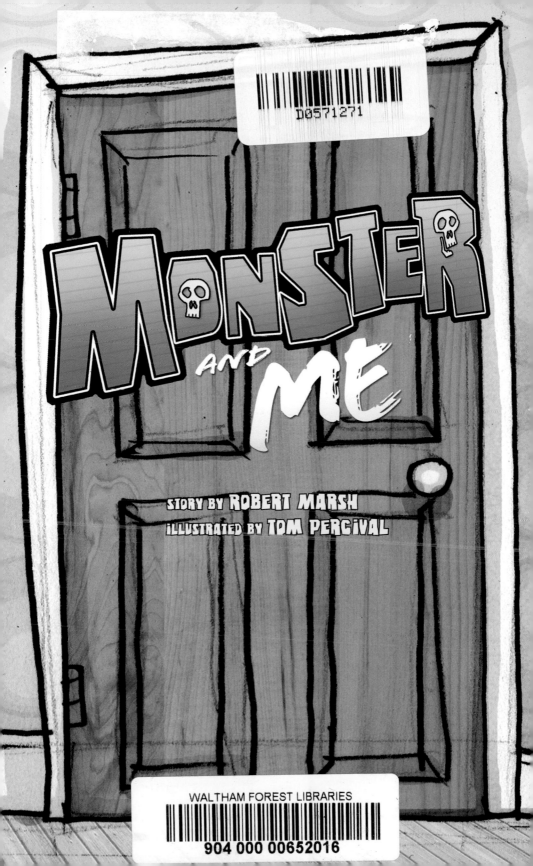

MONSTER AND ME

STORY BY ROBERT MARSH

ILLUSTRATED BY TOM PERCIVAL

Raintree is an imprint of Capstone Global Library Limited, a company incorporated in England and Wales having its registered office at 264 Banbury Road, Oxford, OX2 7DY - Registered company number: 6695582

www.raintree.co.uk
myorders@raintree.co.uk

Creative Director: Heather Kindseth
Designer: Brann Garvey
Production by Tori Abraham
Printed and bound in China

ISBN 978 1 4747 8438 2

British Library Cataloguing in Publication Data
A full catalogue record for this book is available from the British Library.

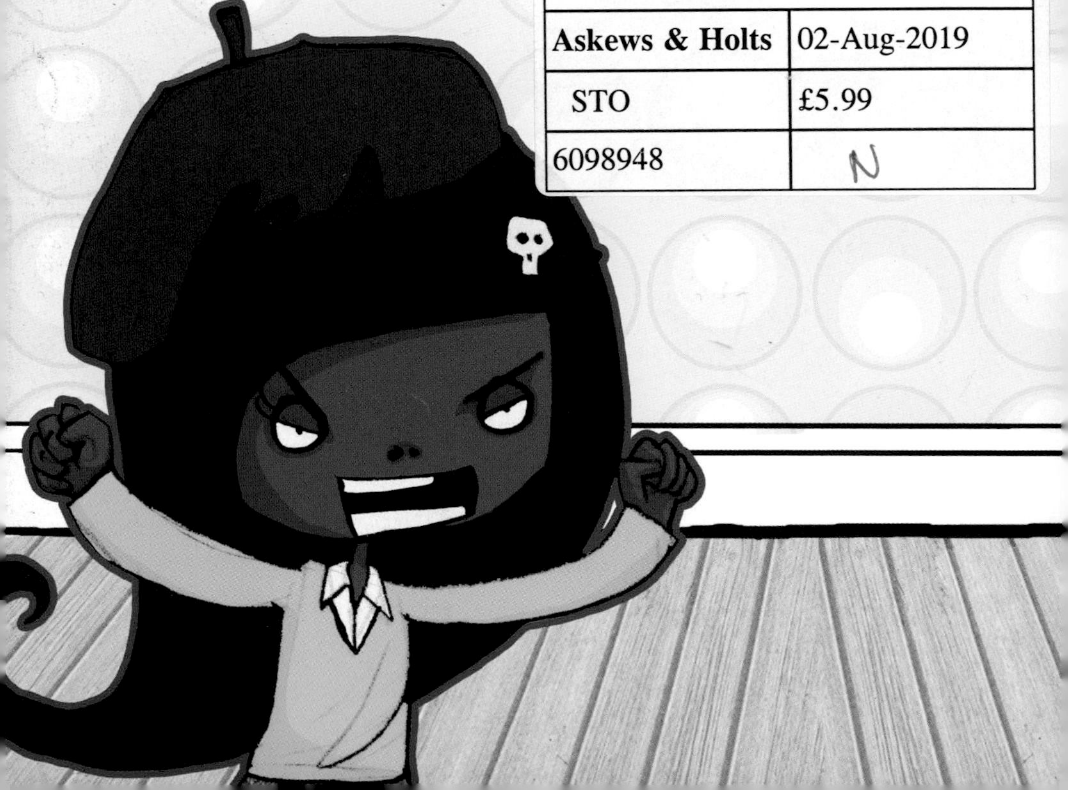

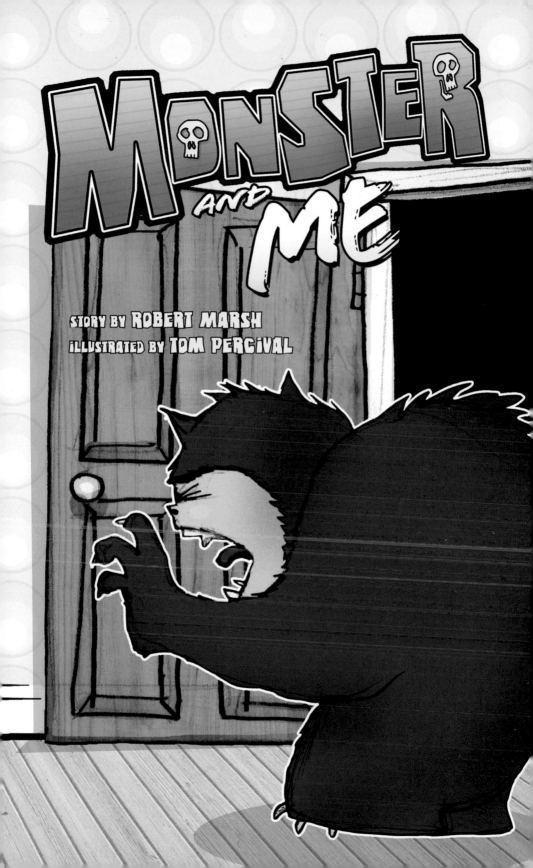

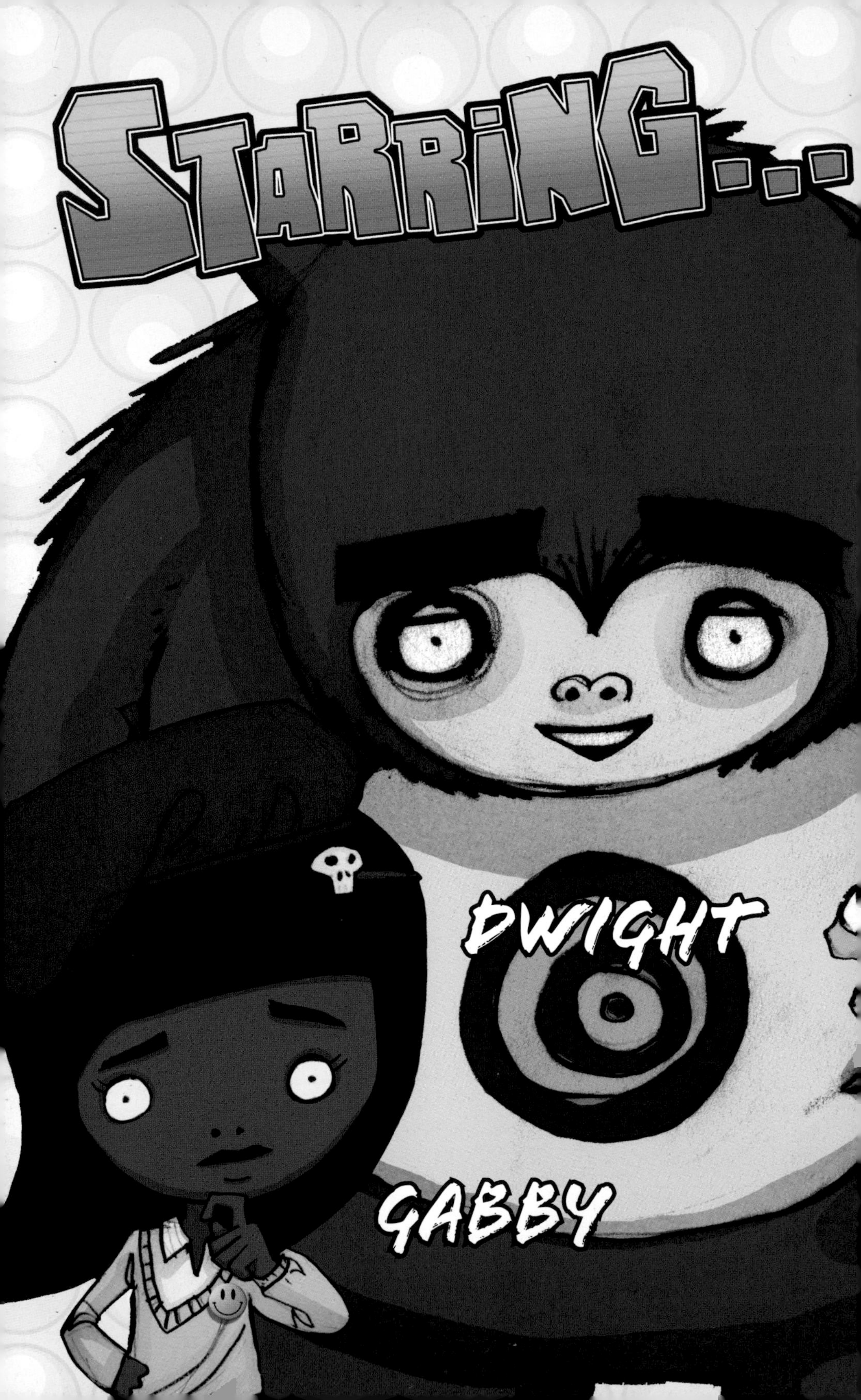
STARRING...
DWIGHT
GABBY

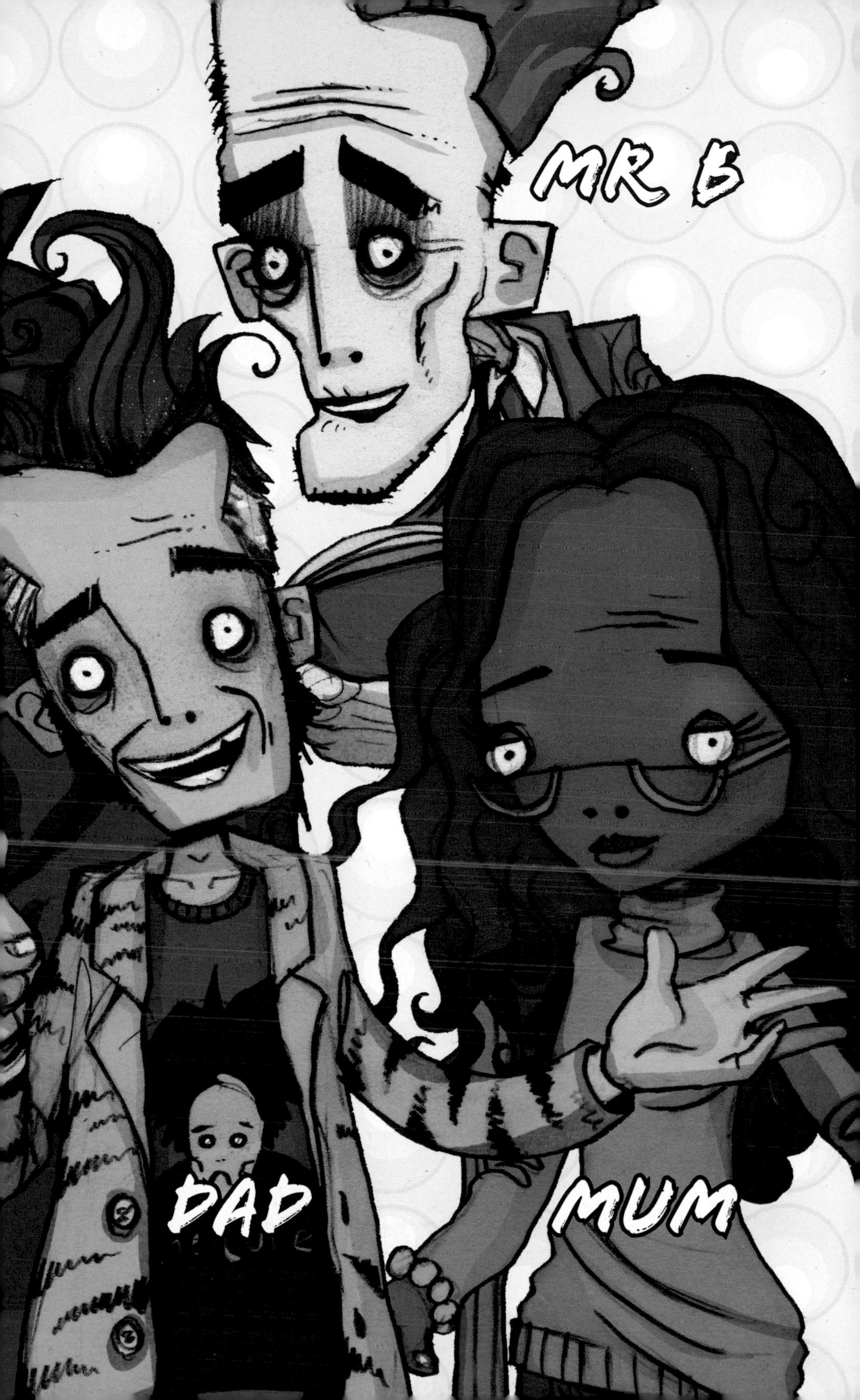
MR B
DAD
MUM

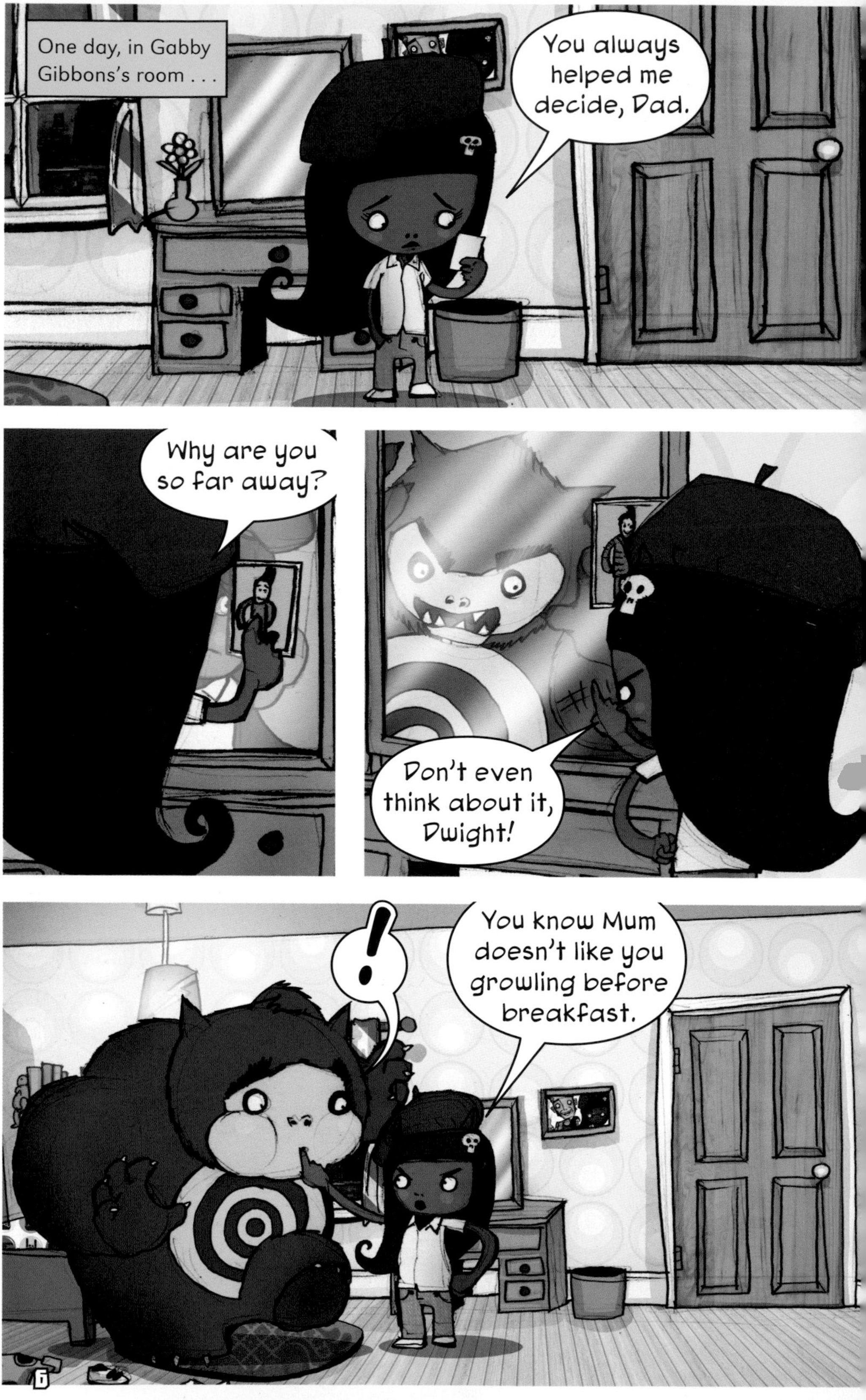
One day, in Gabby Gibbons's room . . .
You always helped me decide, Dad.
Why are you so far away?
Don't even think about it, Dwight!
!
You know Mum doesn't like you growling before breakfast.

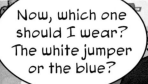

Now, which one should I wear? The white jumper or the blue?

ROaARRR!!

So, the blue one?

7

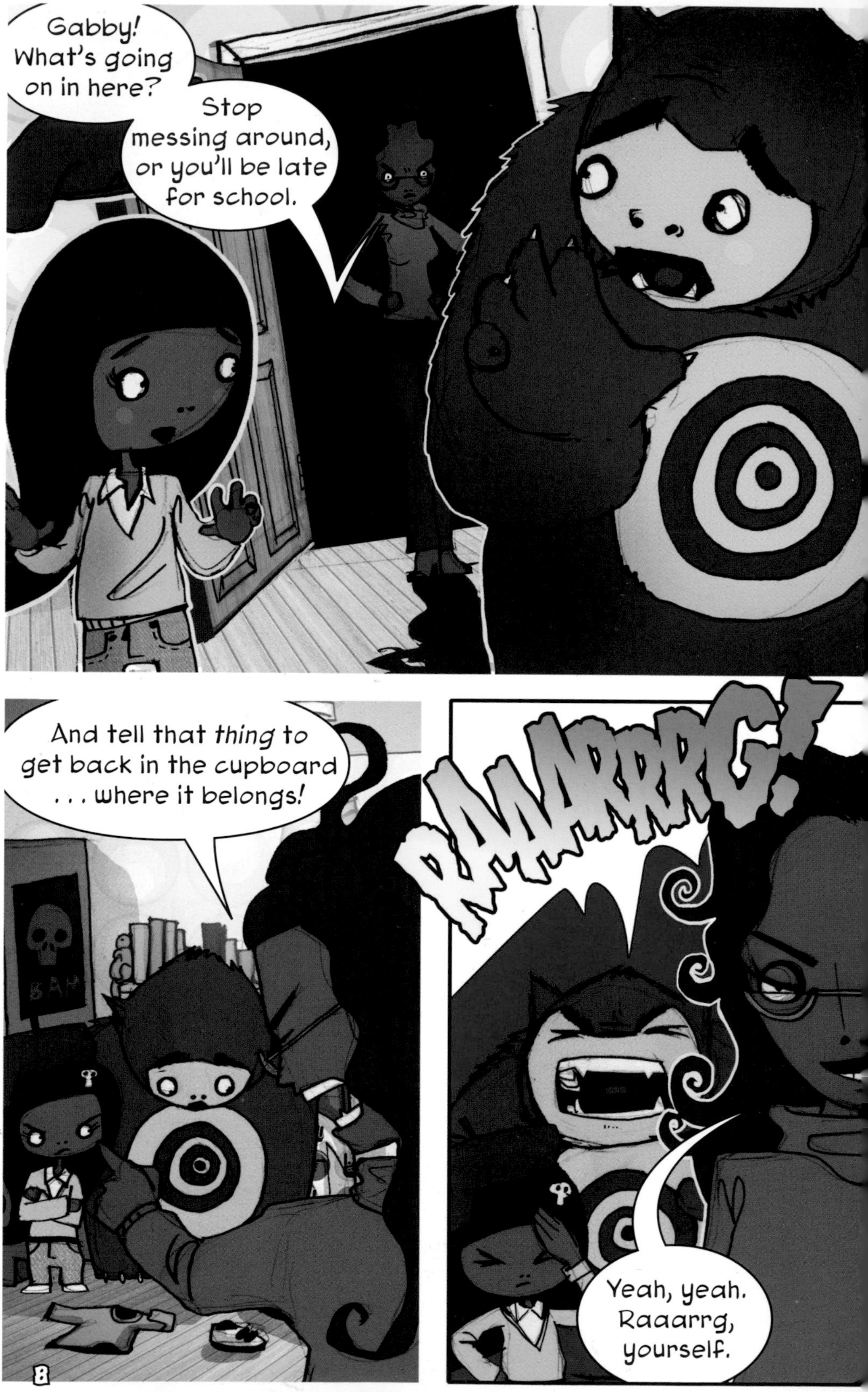
Gabby! What's going on in here?
Stop messing around, or you'll be late for school.
And tell that *thing* to get back in the cupboard . . . where it belongs!
RAAARRRG!
Yeah, yeah. Raaarrg, yourself.

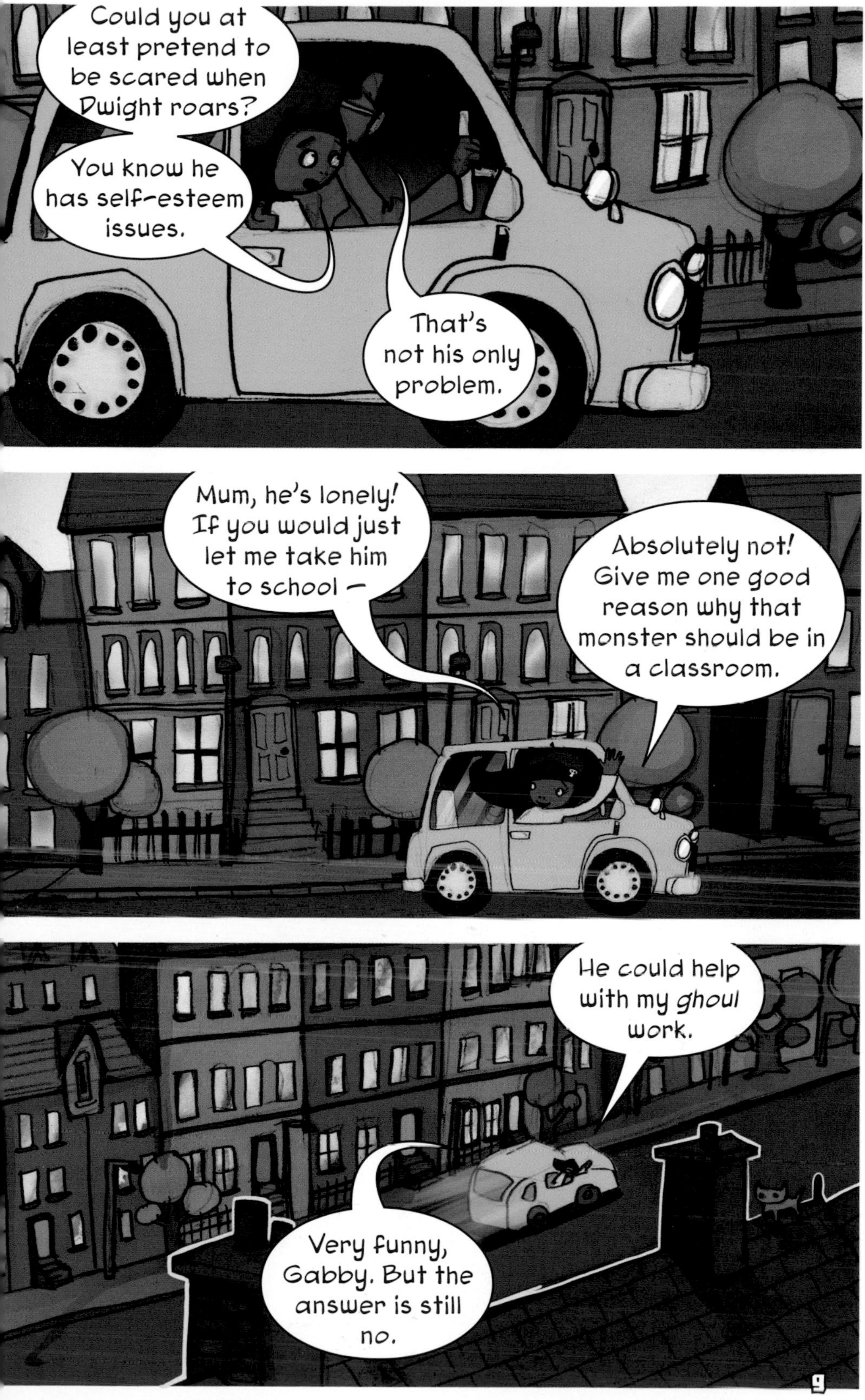
Could you at least pretend to be scared when Dwight roars?
You know he has self-esteem issues.
That's not his only problem.
Mum, he's lonely! If you would just let me take him to school –
Absolutely not! Give me one good reason why that monster should be in a classroom.
He could help with my *ghoul* work.
Very funny, Gabby. But the answer is still no.

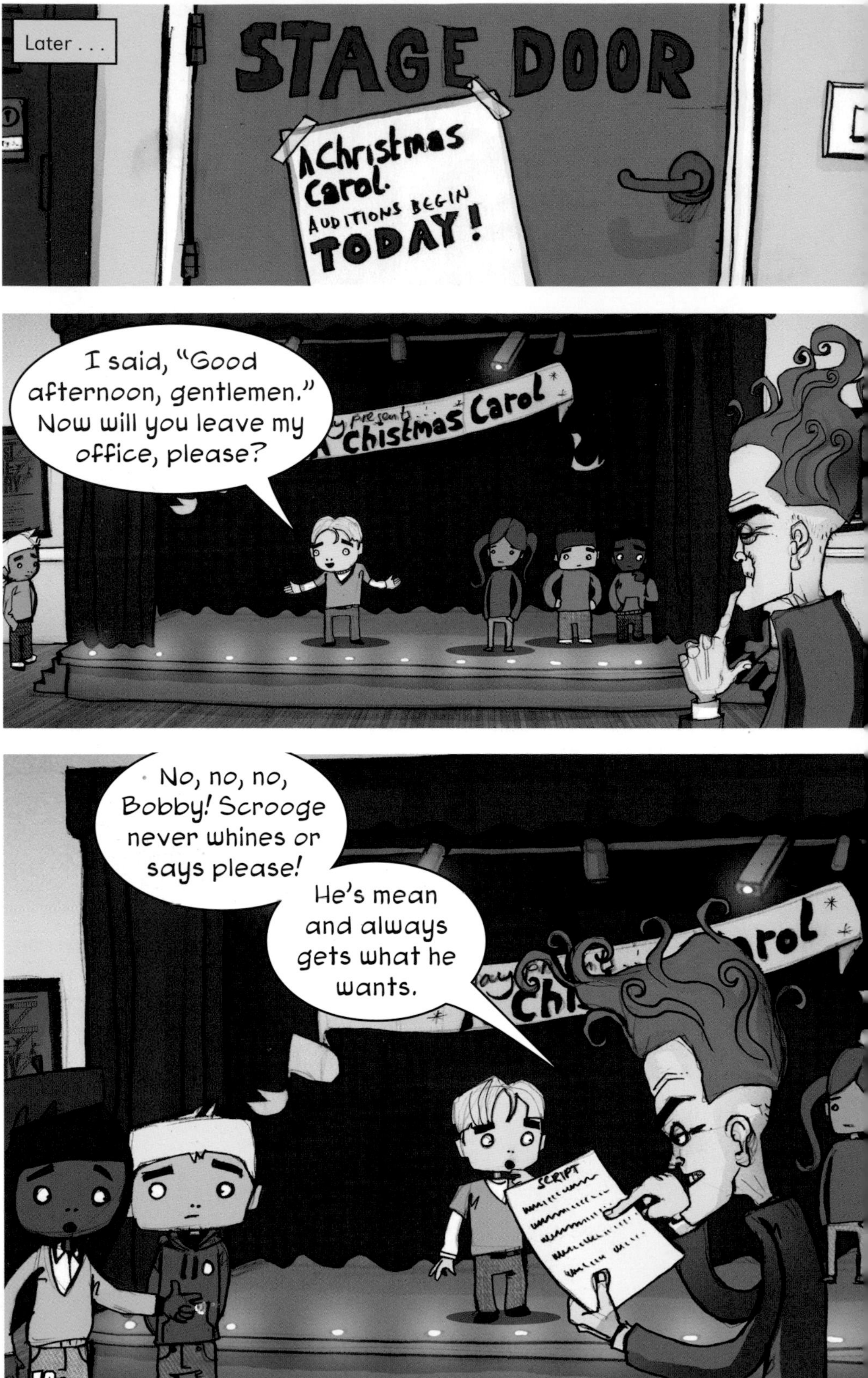
Later . . .
STAGE DOOR
A Christmas Carol.
AUDITIONS BEGIN TODAY!
Chistmas Carol
I said, "Good afternoon, gentlemen." Now will you leave my office, please?
No, no, no, Bobby! Scrooge never whines or says please!
He's mean and always gets what he wants.
SCRIPT

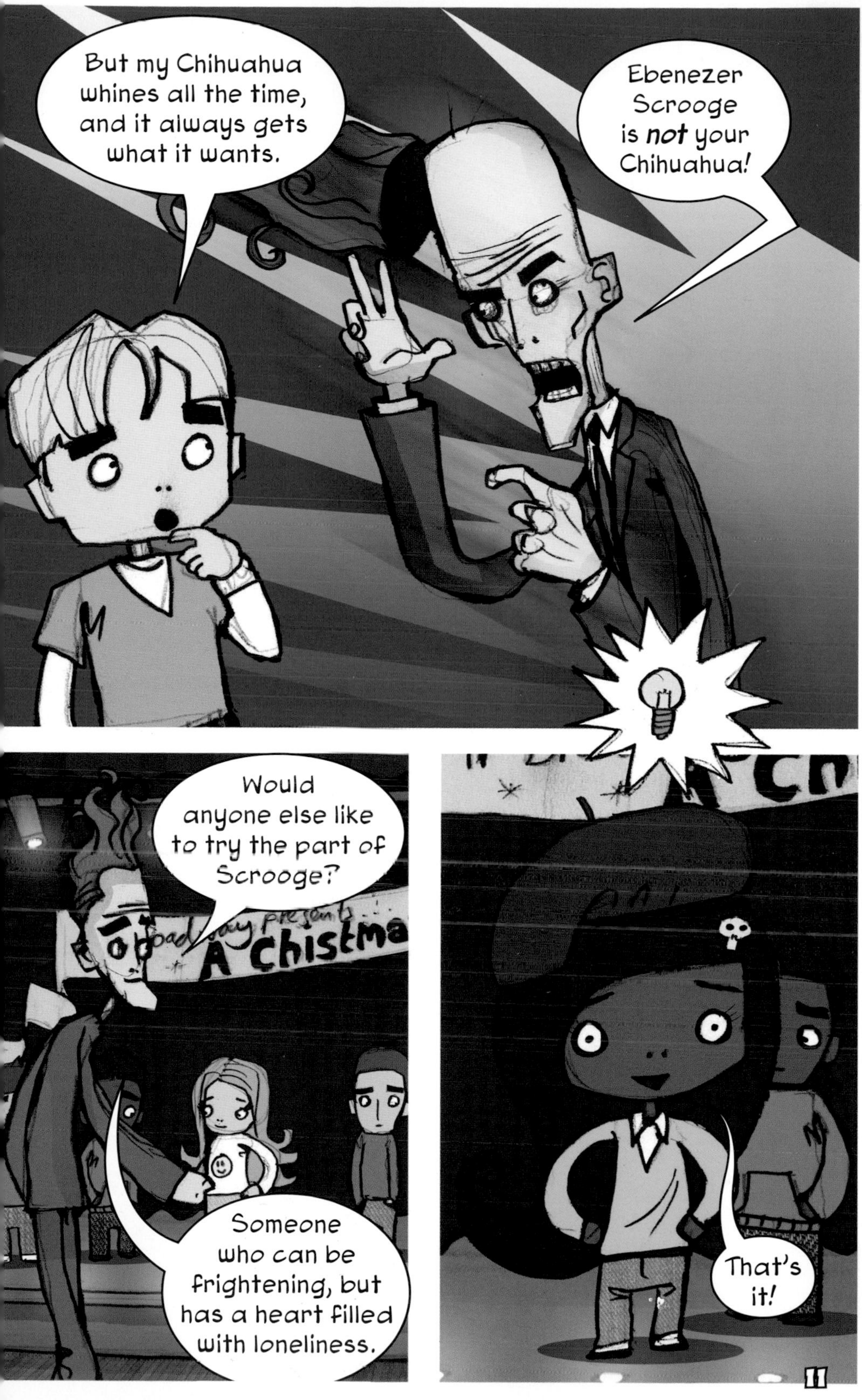
But my Chihuahua whines all the time, and it always gets what it wants.
Ebenezer Scrooge is **not** your Chihuahua!
Would anyone else like to try the part of Scrooge?
Someone who can be frightening, but has a heart filled with loneliness.
That's it!

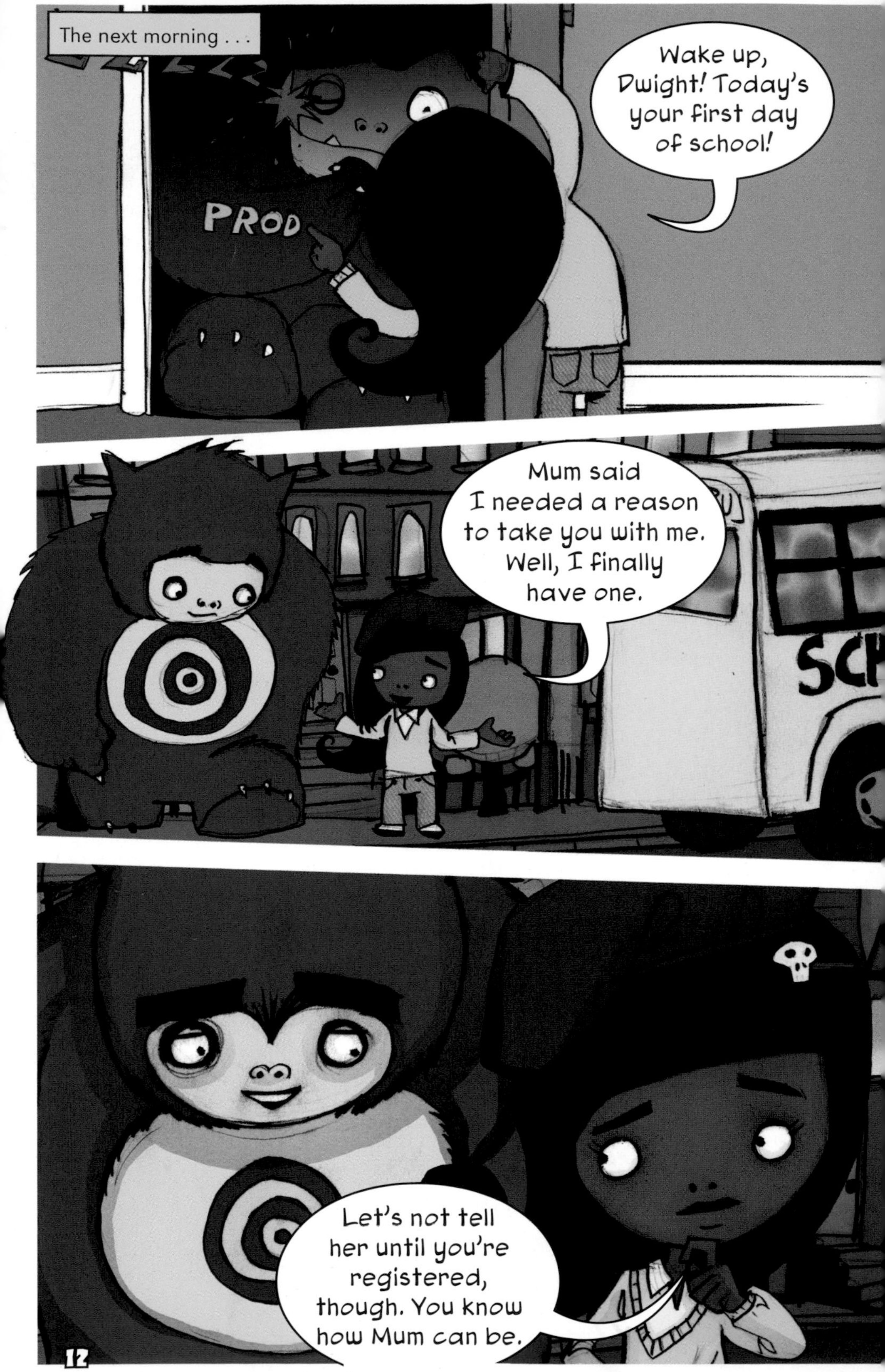
The next morning . . .
PROD
Wake up, Dwight! Today's your first day of school!
Mum said I needed a reason to take you with me. Well, I finally have one.
Let's not tell her until you're registered, though. You know how Mum can be.

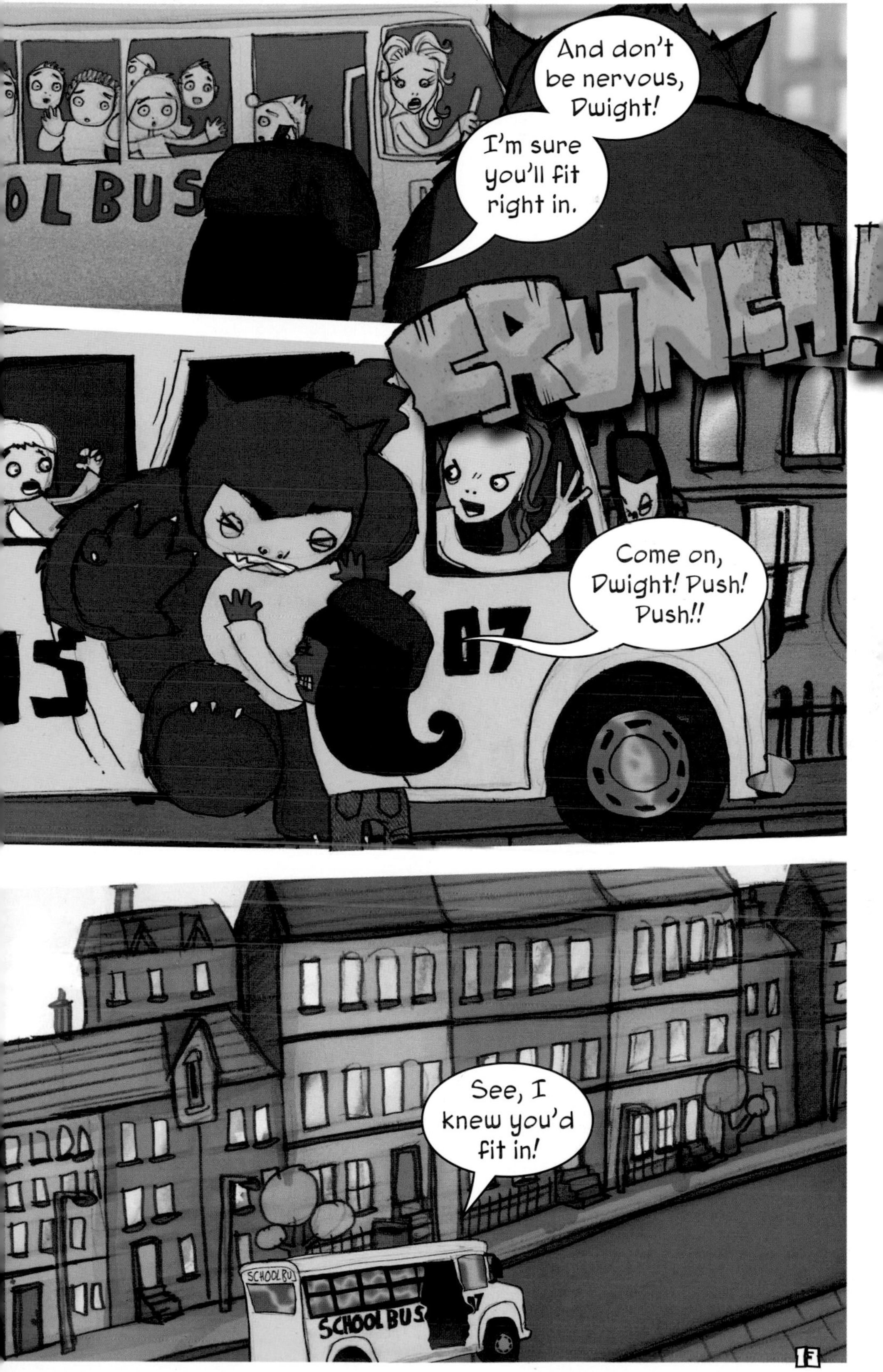
And don't be nervous, Dwight!
I'm sure you'll fit right in.
CRUNCH!
Come on, Dwight! Push! Push!!
SCHOOL BUS
See, I knew you'd fit in!

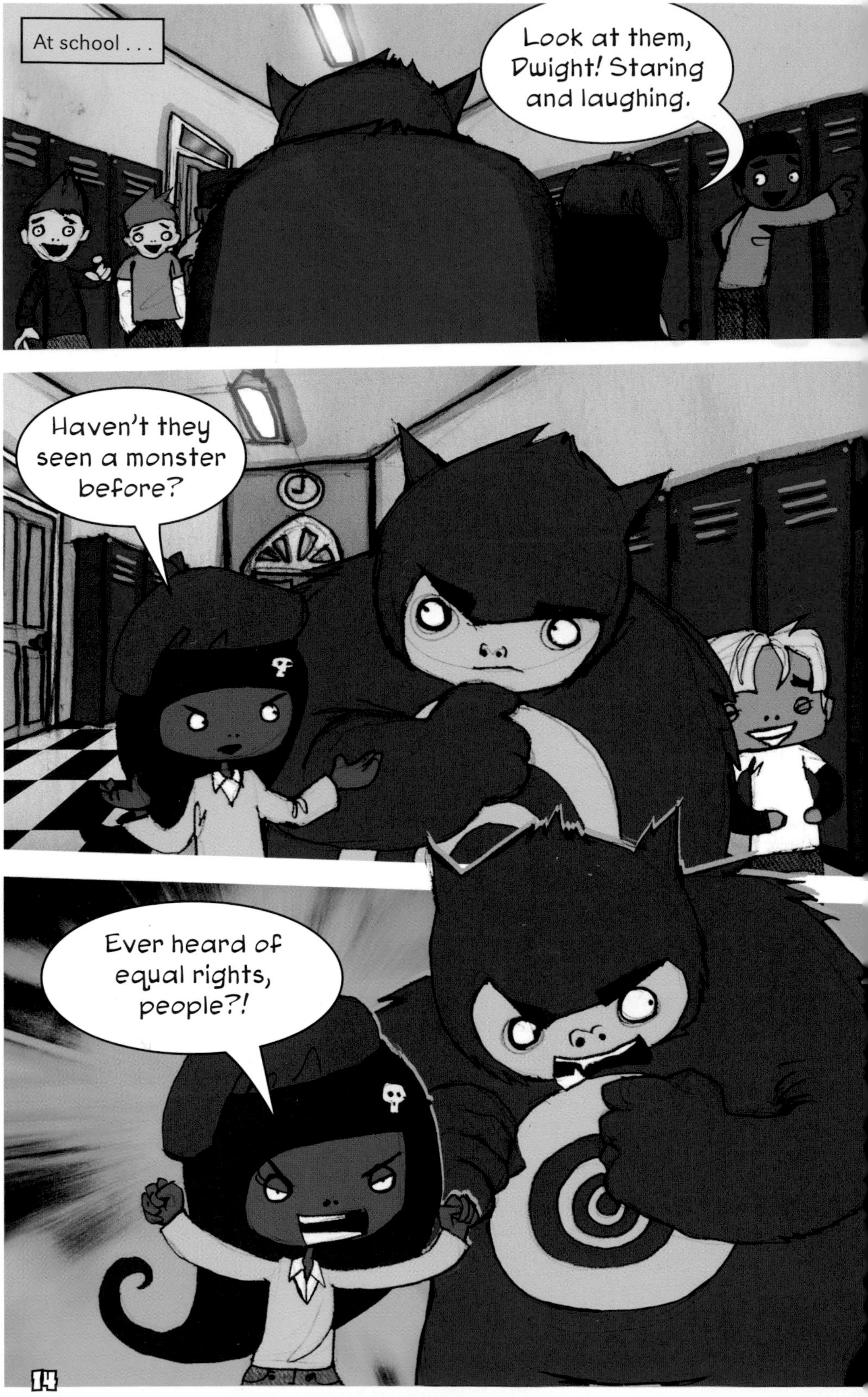
At school . . .
Look at them, Dwight! Staring and laughing.
Haven't they seen a monster before?
Ever heard of equal rights, people?!

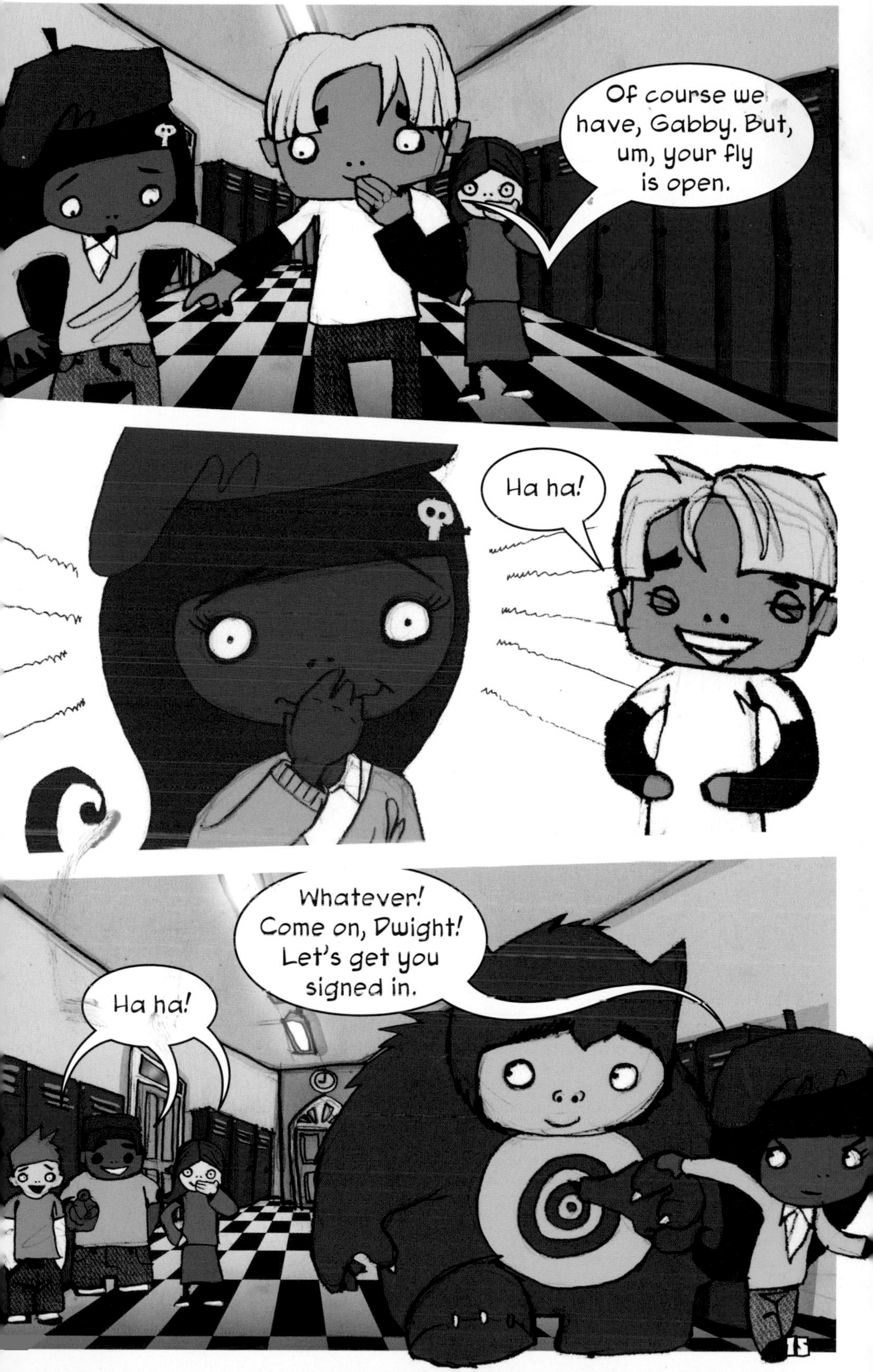
Of course we have, Gabby. But, um, your fly is open.
Ha ha!
Whatever! Come on, Dwight! Let's get you signed in.
Ha ha!

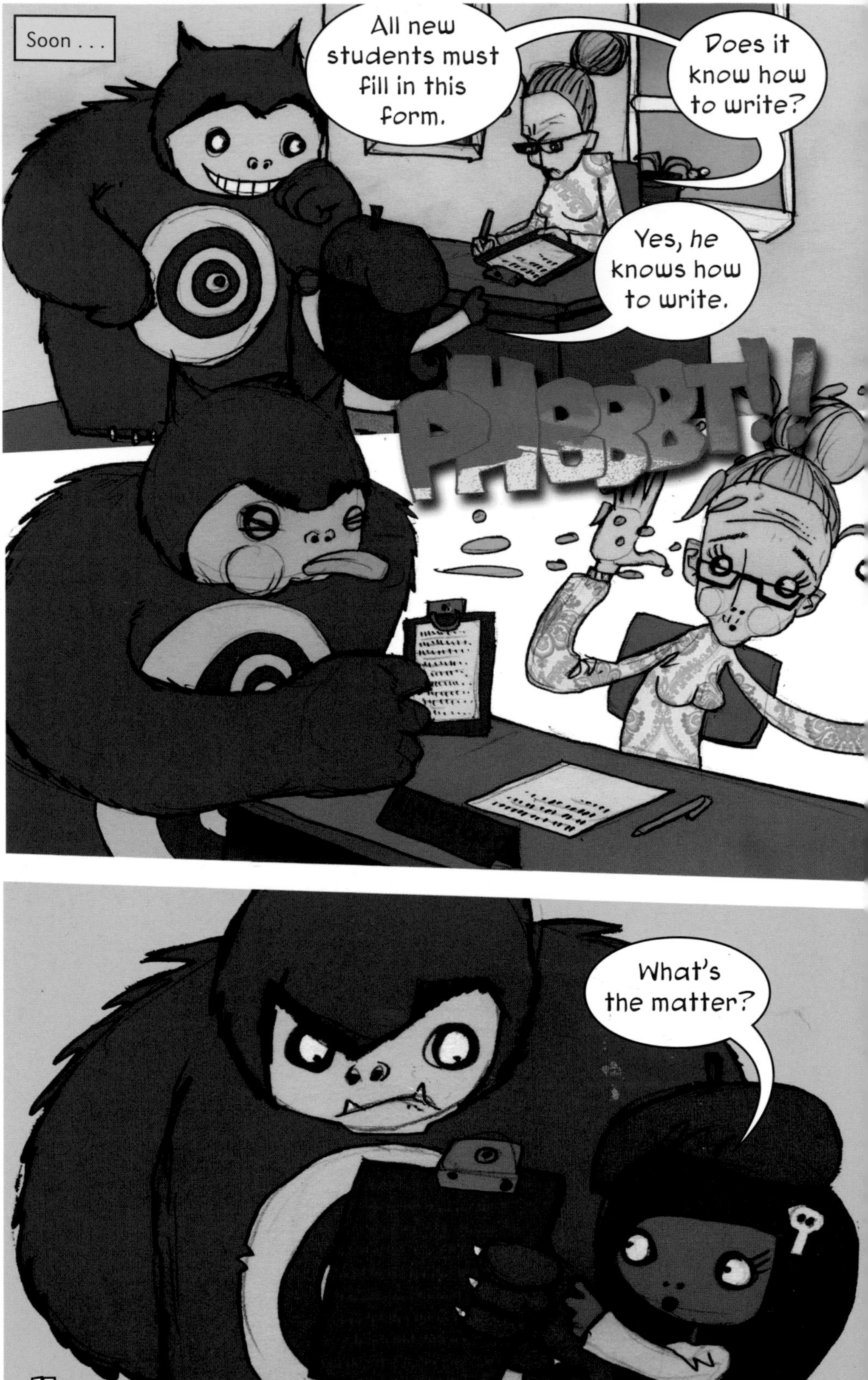

Soon . . .
All new students must fill in this form.
Does it know how to write?
Yes, he knows how to write.
PHBBT!!
What's the matter?

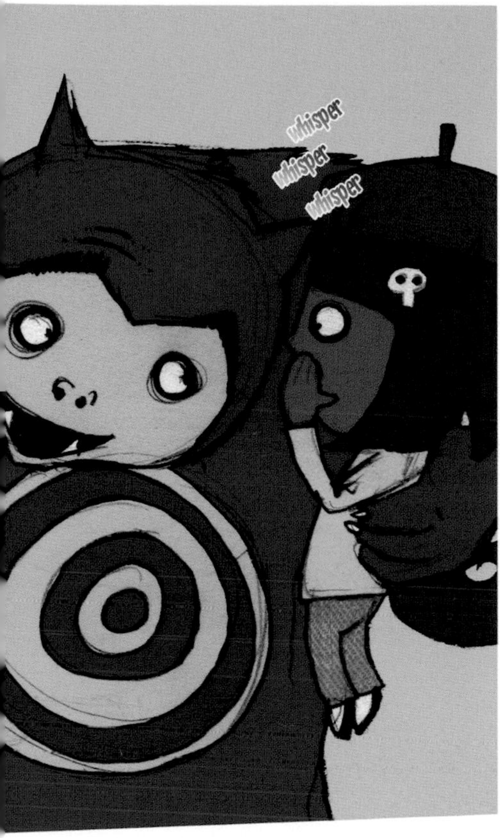
whisper
whisper
whisper

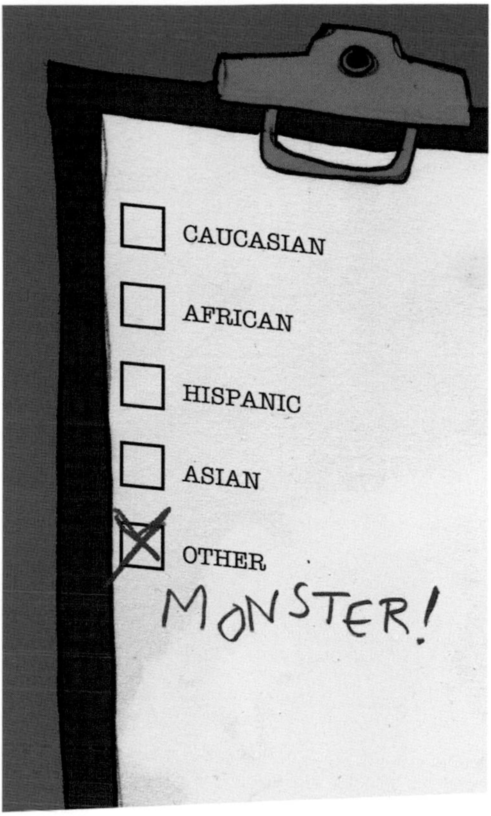
CAUCASIAN
AFRICAN
HISPANIC
ASIAN
OTHER
MONSTER!

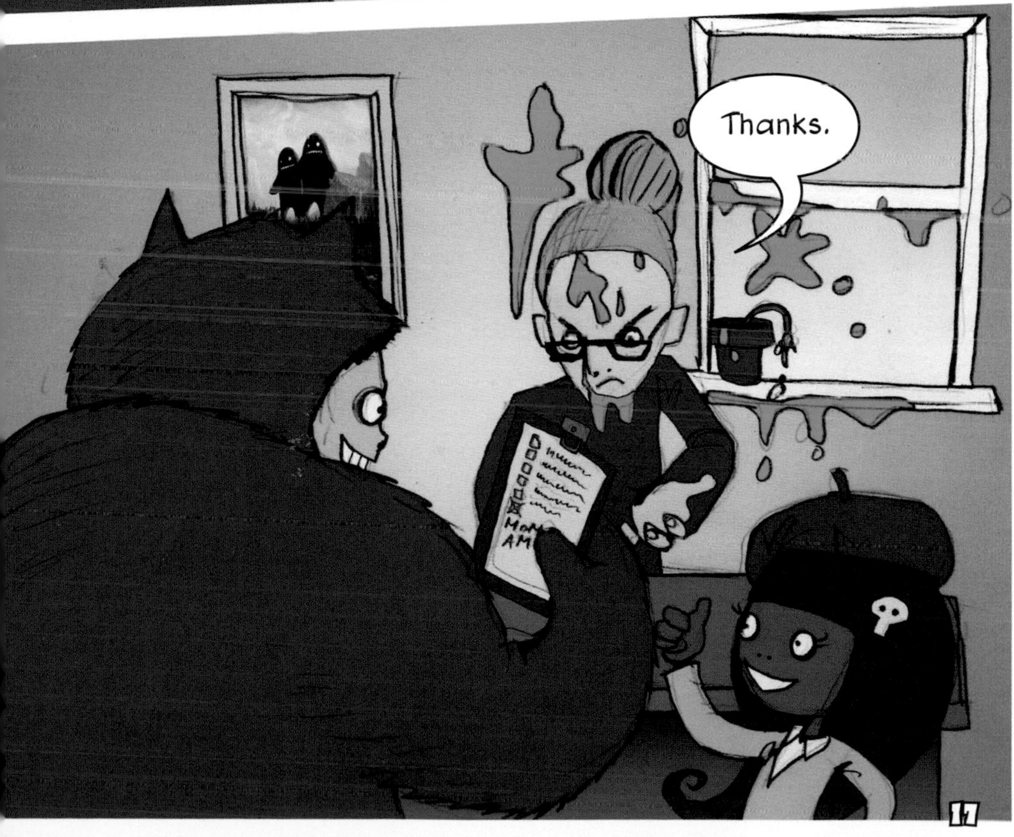
Thanks.

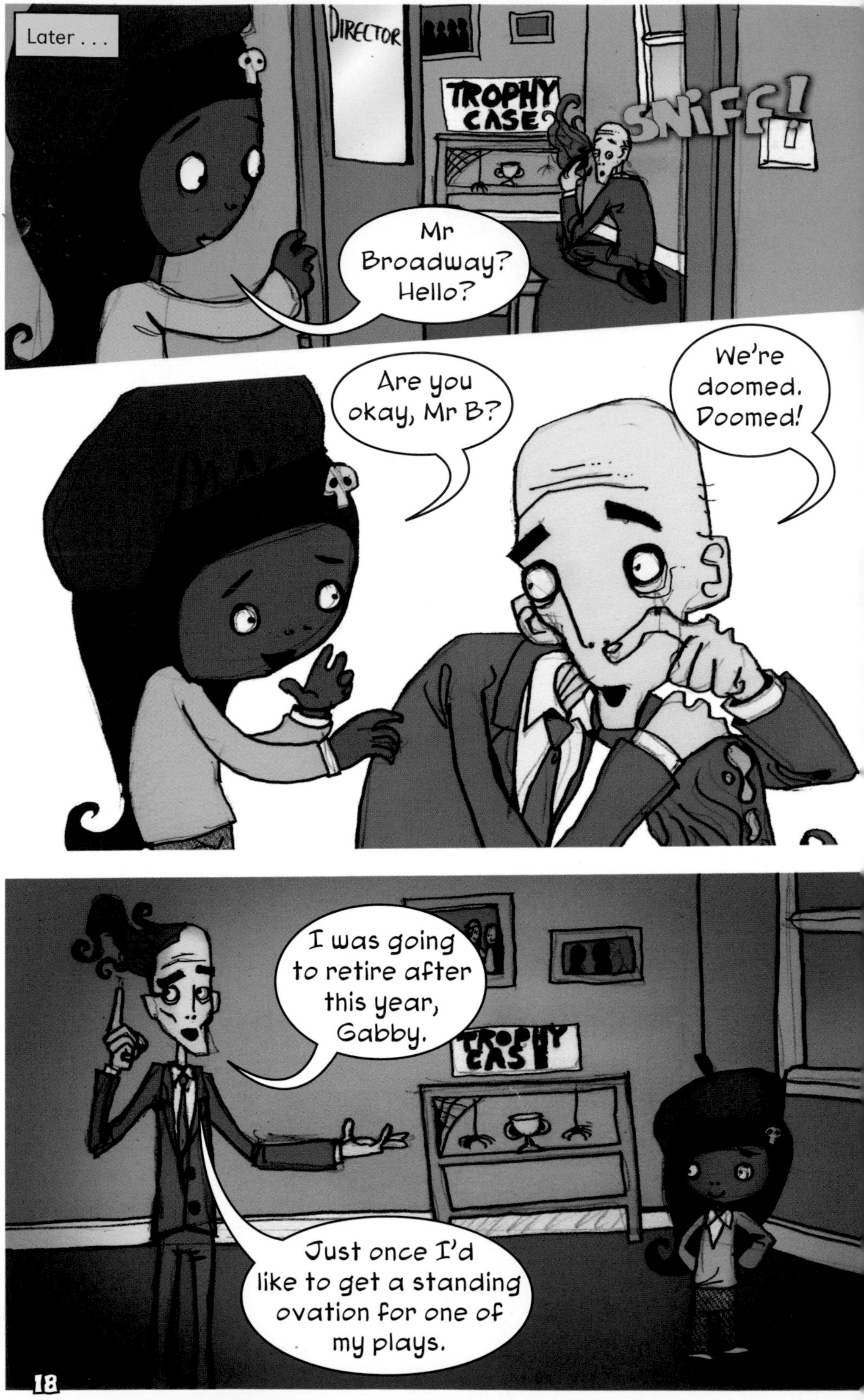
Later . . .
DIRECTOR
TROPHY CASE
SNIFF!
Mr Broadway? Hello?
Are you okay, Mr B?
We're doomed. Doomed!
TROPHY CASE
I was going to retire after this year, Gabby.
Just once I'd like to get a standing ovation for one of my plays.

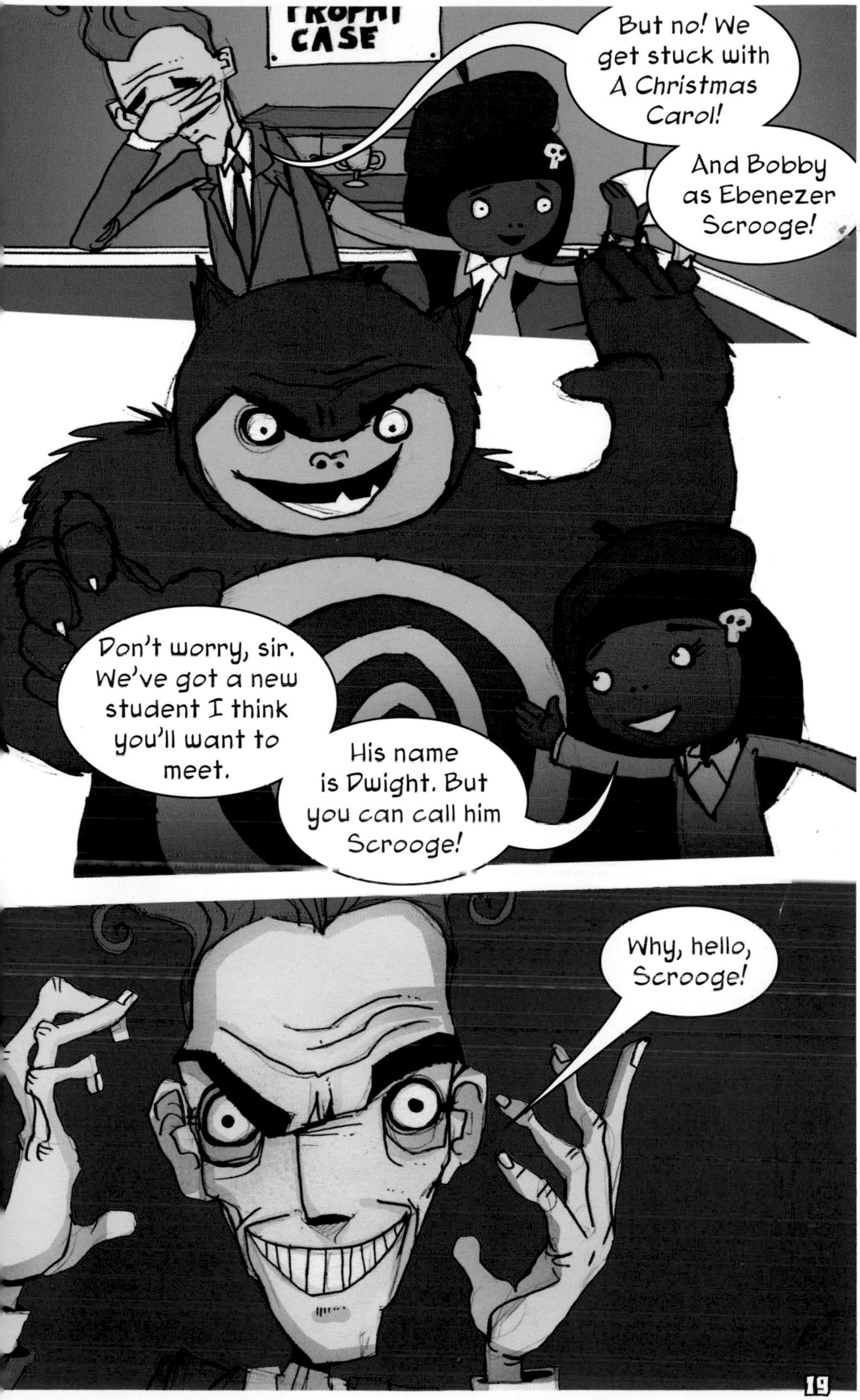
TROPHY CASE
But no! We get stuck with A Christmas Carol!
And Bobby as Ebenezer Scrooge!
Don't worry, sir. We've got a new student I think you'll want to meet.
His name is Dwight. But you can call him Scrooge!
Why, hello, Scrooge!

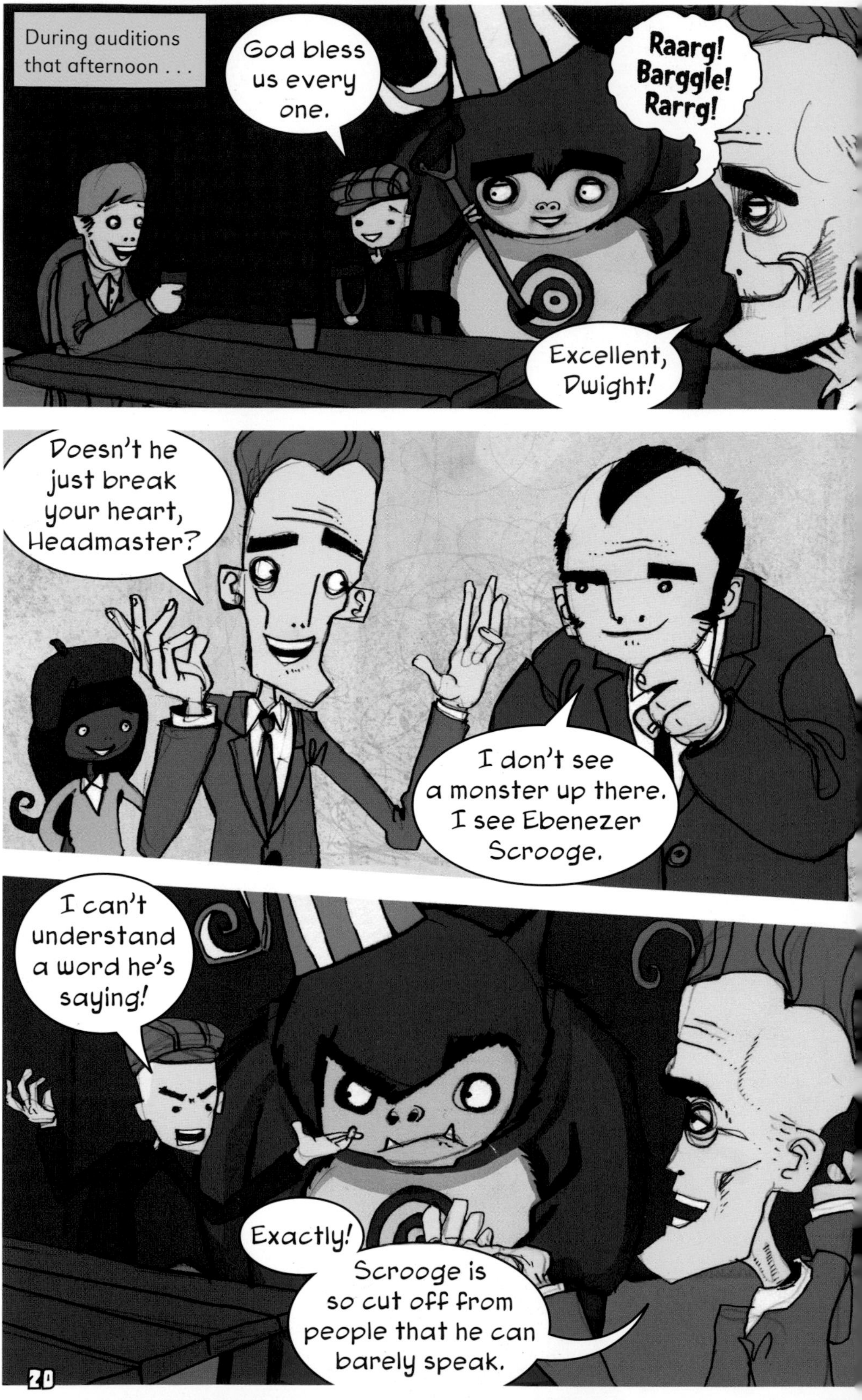
During auditions that afternoon . . .
God bless us every one.
Raarg! Barggle! Rarrg!
Excellent, Dwight!
Doesn't he just break your heart, Headmaster?
I don't see a monster up there. I see Ebenezer Scrooge.
I can't understand a word he's saying!
Exactly!
Scrooge is so cut off from people that he can barely speak.

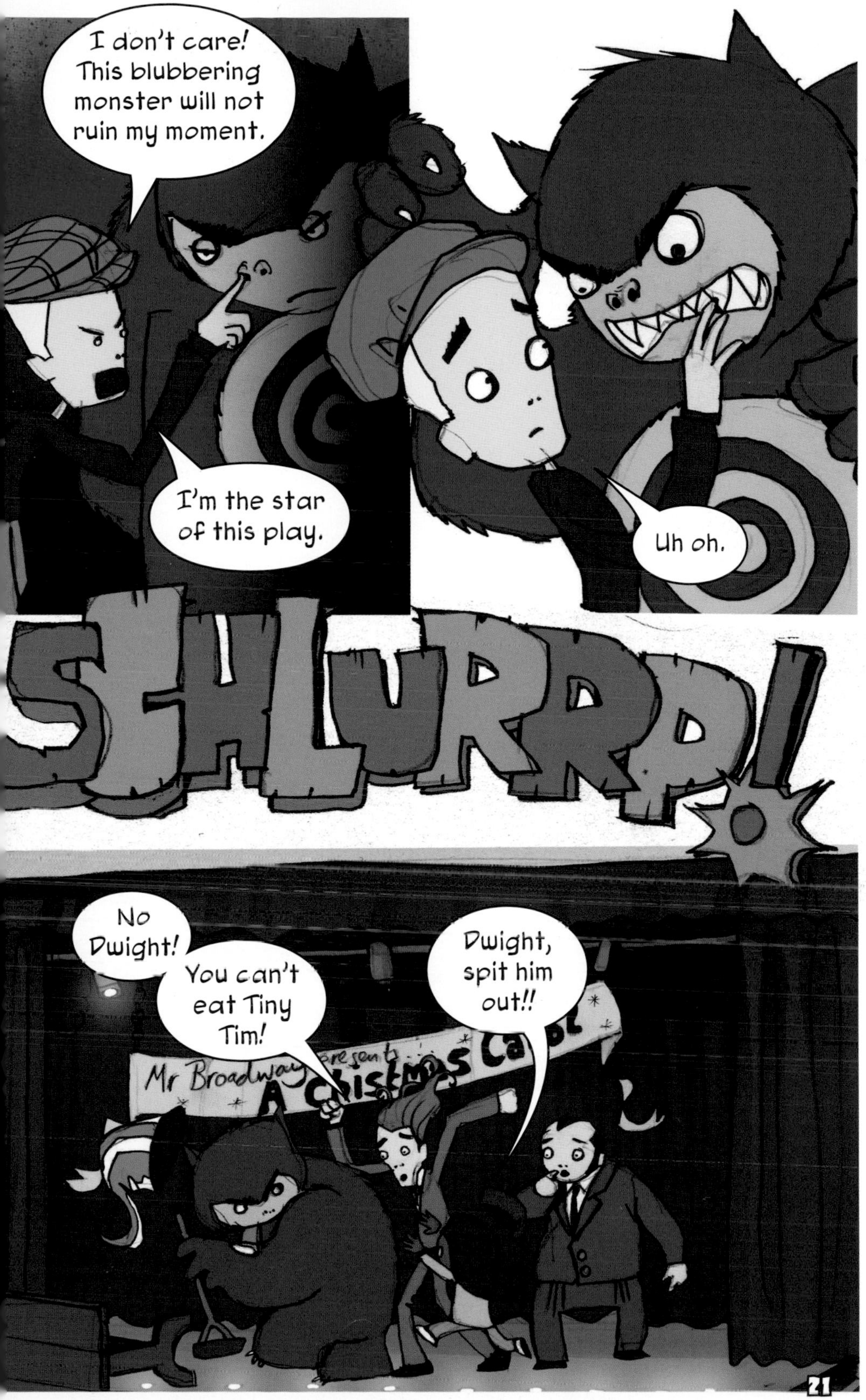
I don't care! This blubbering monster will not ruin my moment.
I'm the star of this play.
Uh oh.
SCHLURRP!
No Dwight!
You can't eat Tiny Tim!
Dwight, spit him out!!
Mr Broadway

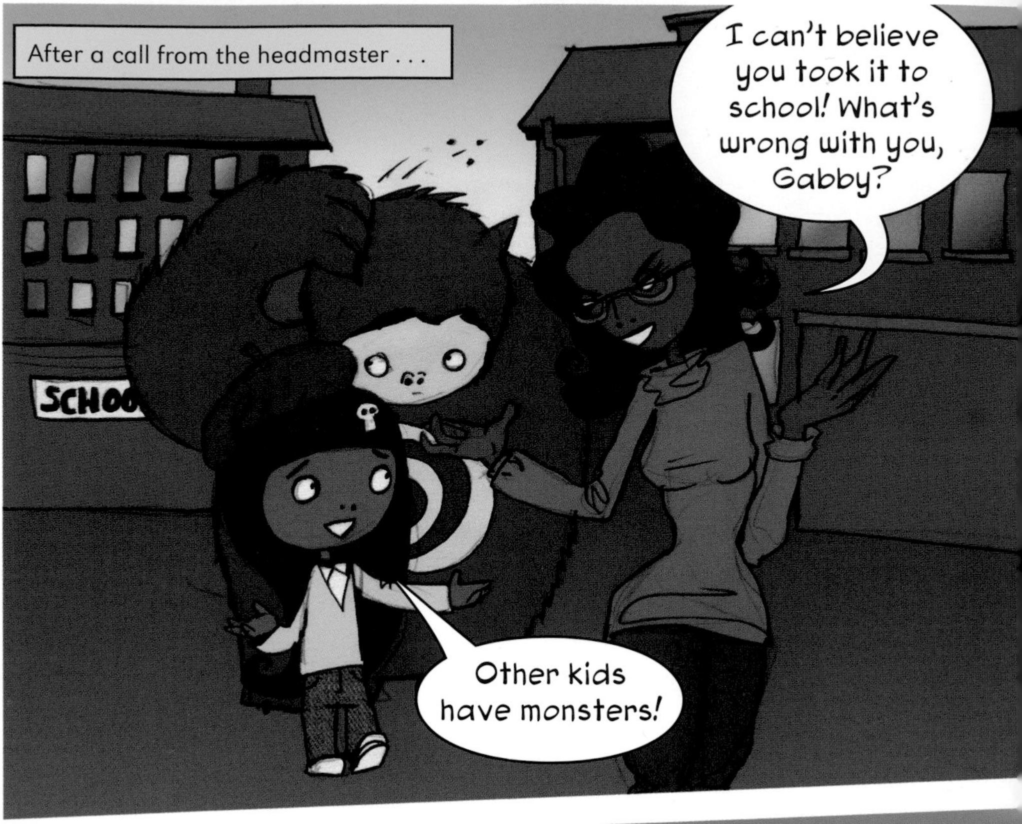
After a call from the headmaster . . .
I can't believe you took it to school! What's wrong with you, Gabby?
SCHOO
Other kids have monsters!

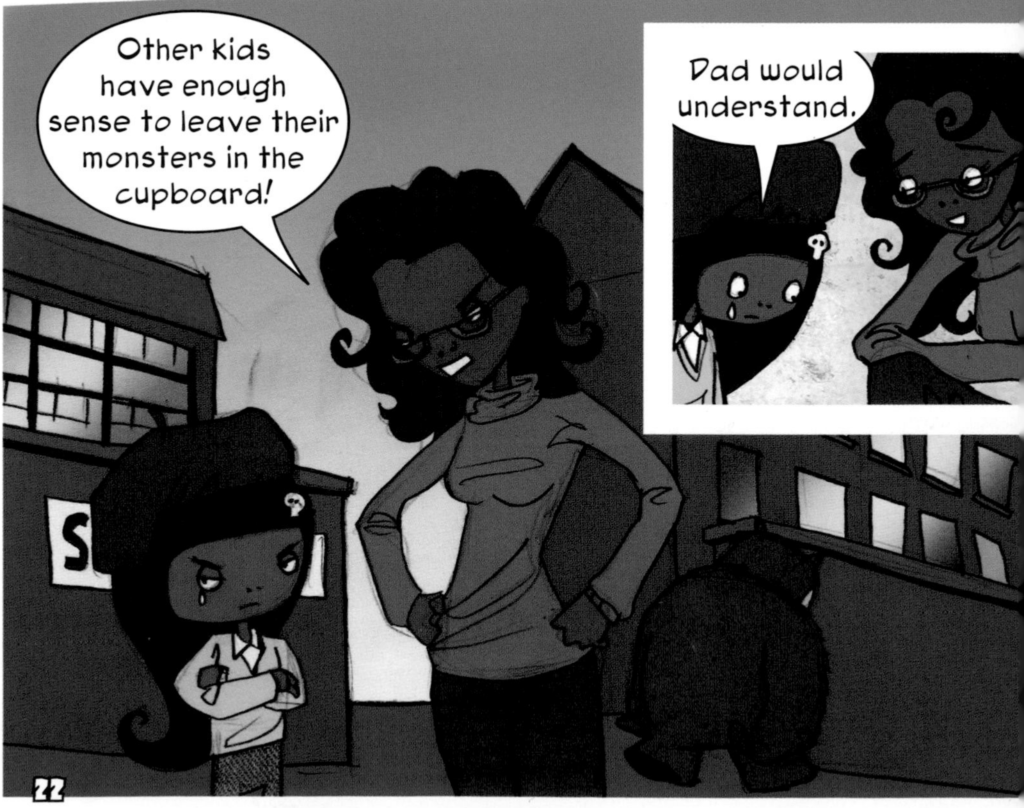
Other kids have enough sense to leave their monsters in the cupboard!
Dad would understand.

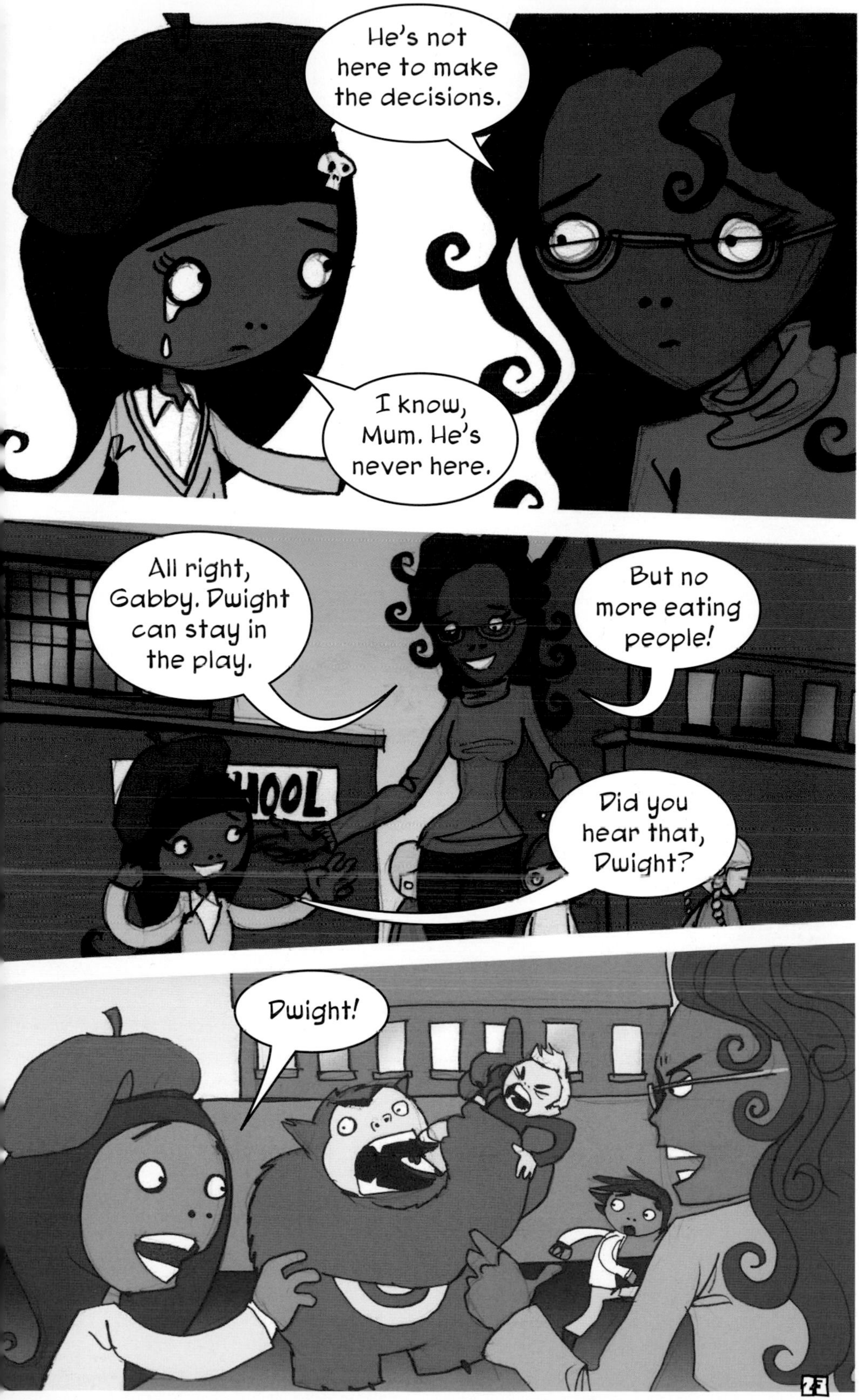
He's not here to make the decisions.
I know, Mum. He's never here.
All right, Gabby. Dwight can stay in the play.
But no more eating people!
SCHOOL
Did you hear that, Dwight?
Dwight!

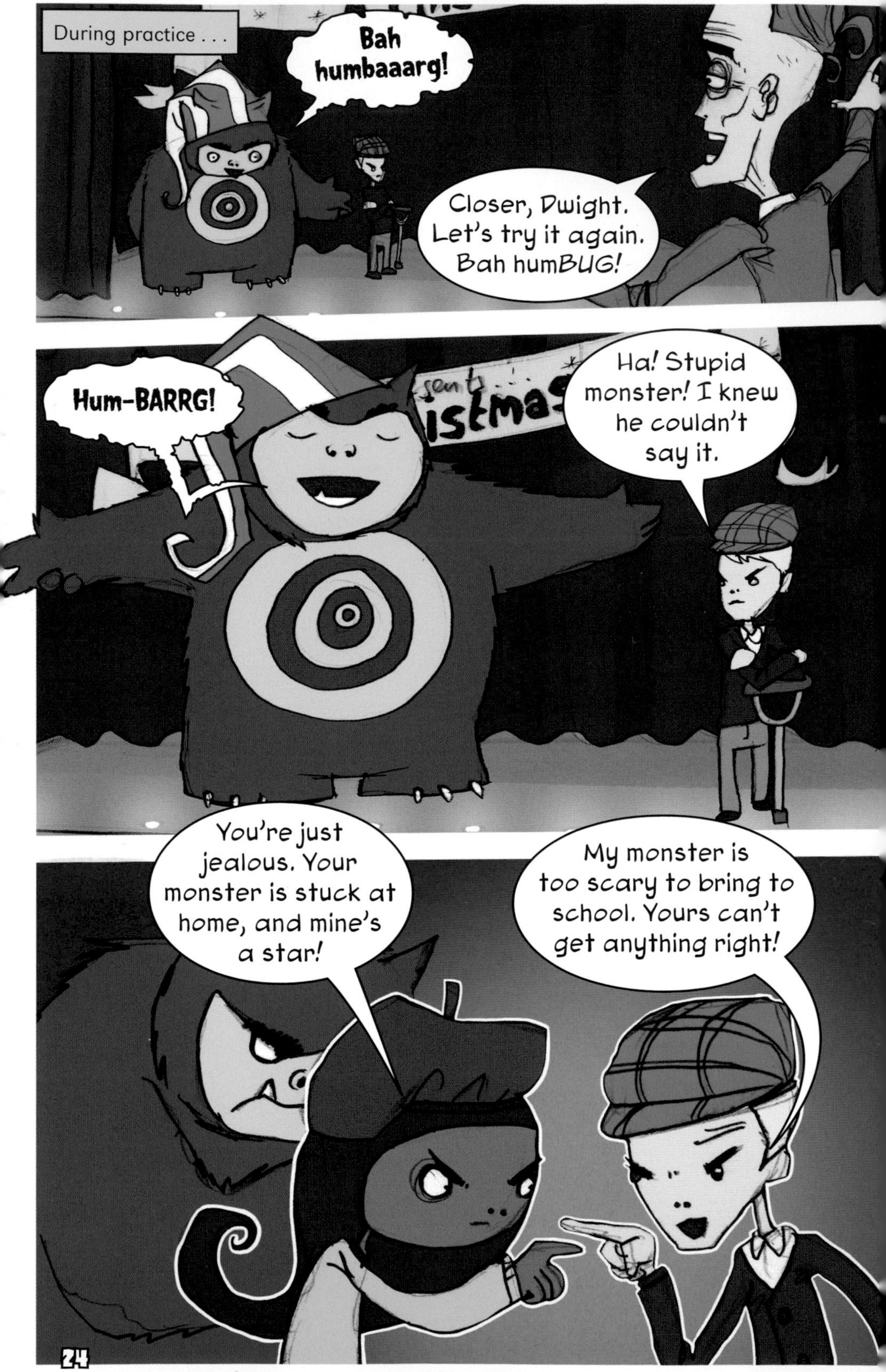
During practice . . .
Bah humbaaarg!
Closer, Dwight. Let's try it again. Bah humBUG!
Hum-BARRG!
Ha! Stupid monster! I knew he couldn't say it.
You're just jealous. Your monster is stuck at home, and mine's a star!
My monster is too scary to bring to school. Yours can't get anything right!

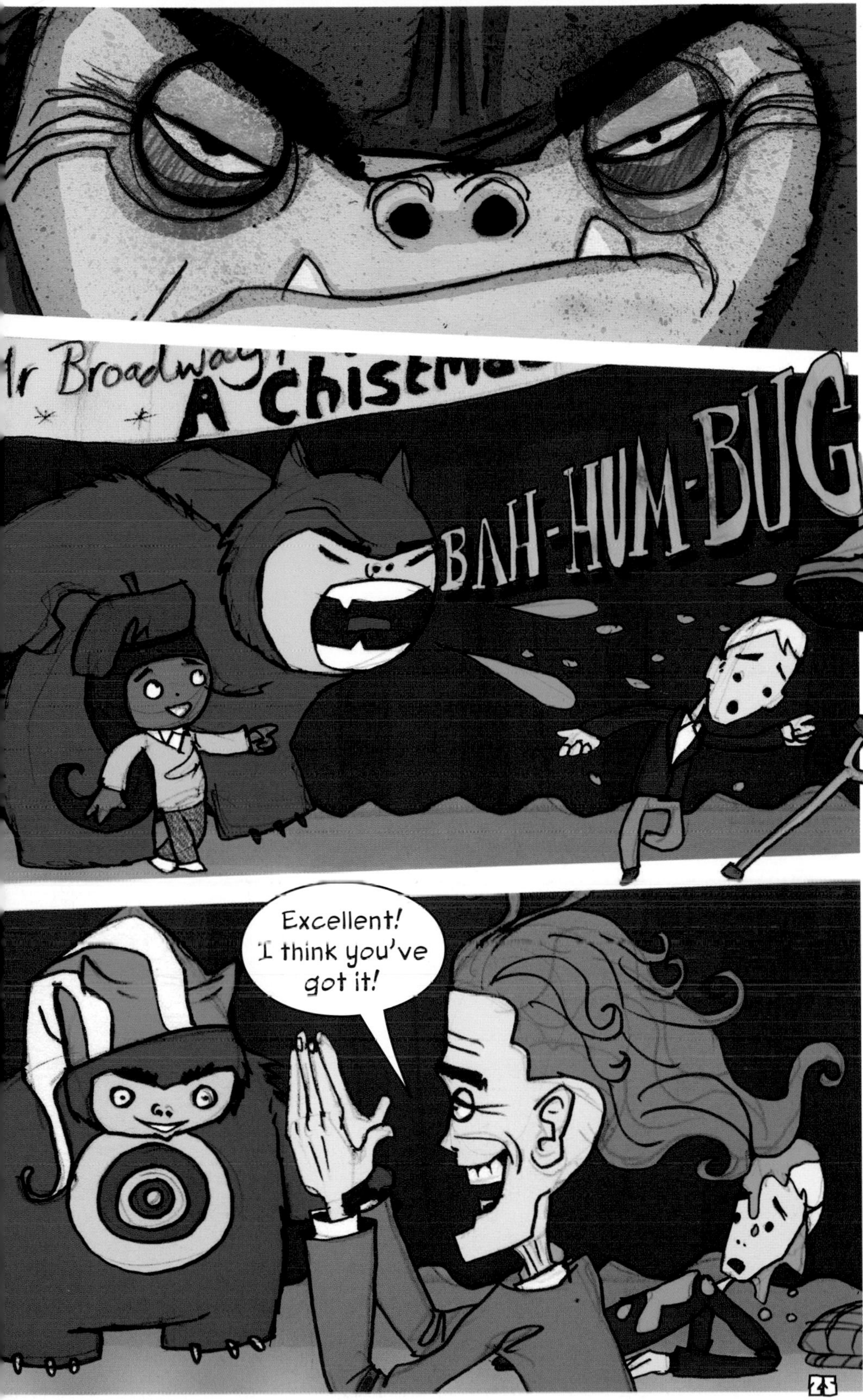
BAH-HUM-BUG!
Excellent! I think you've got it!

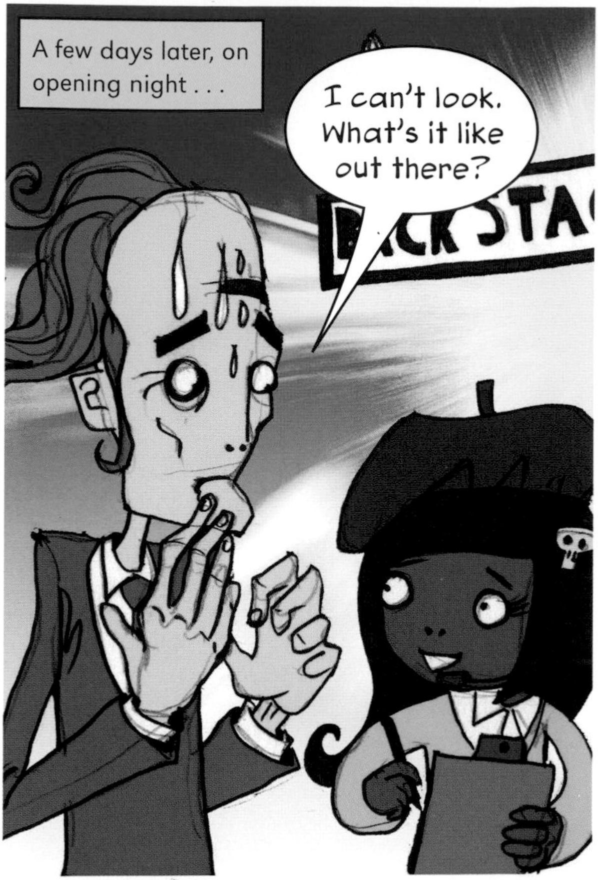
A few days later, on opening night . . .
I can't look. What's it like out there?

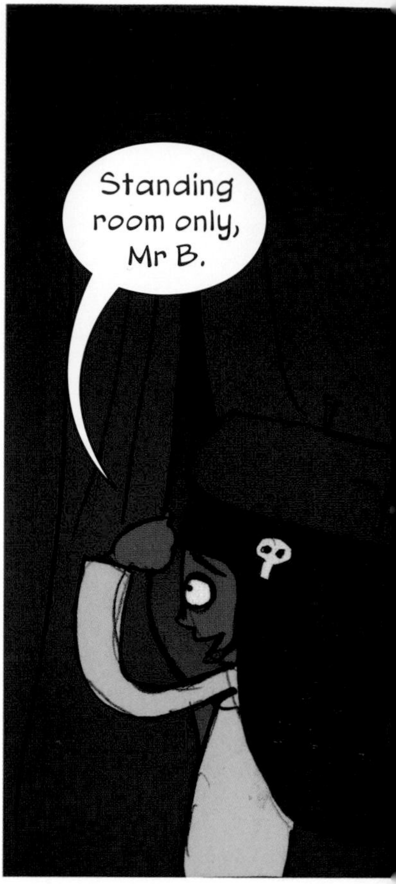
Standing room only, Mr B.

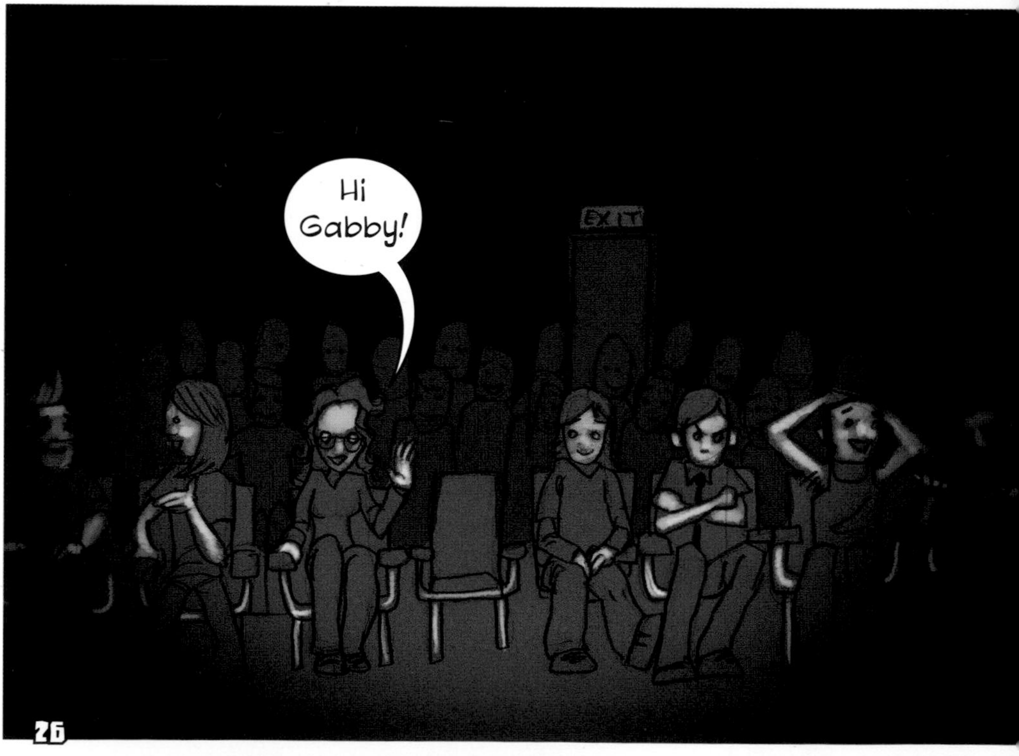
Hi Gabby!
EXIT

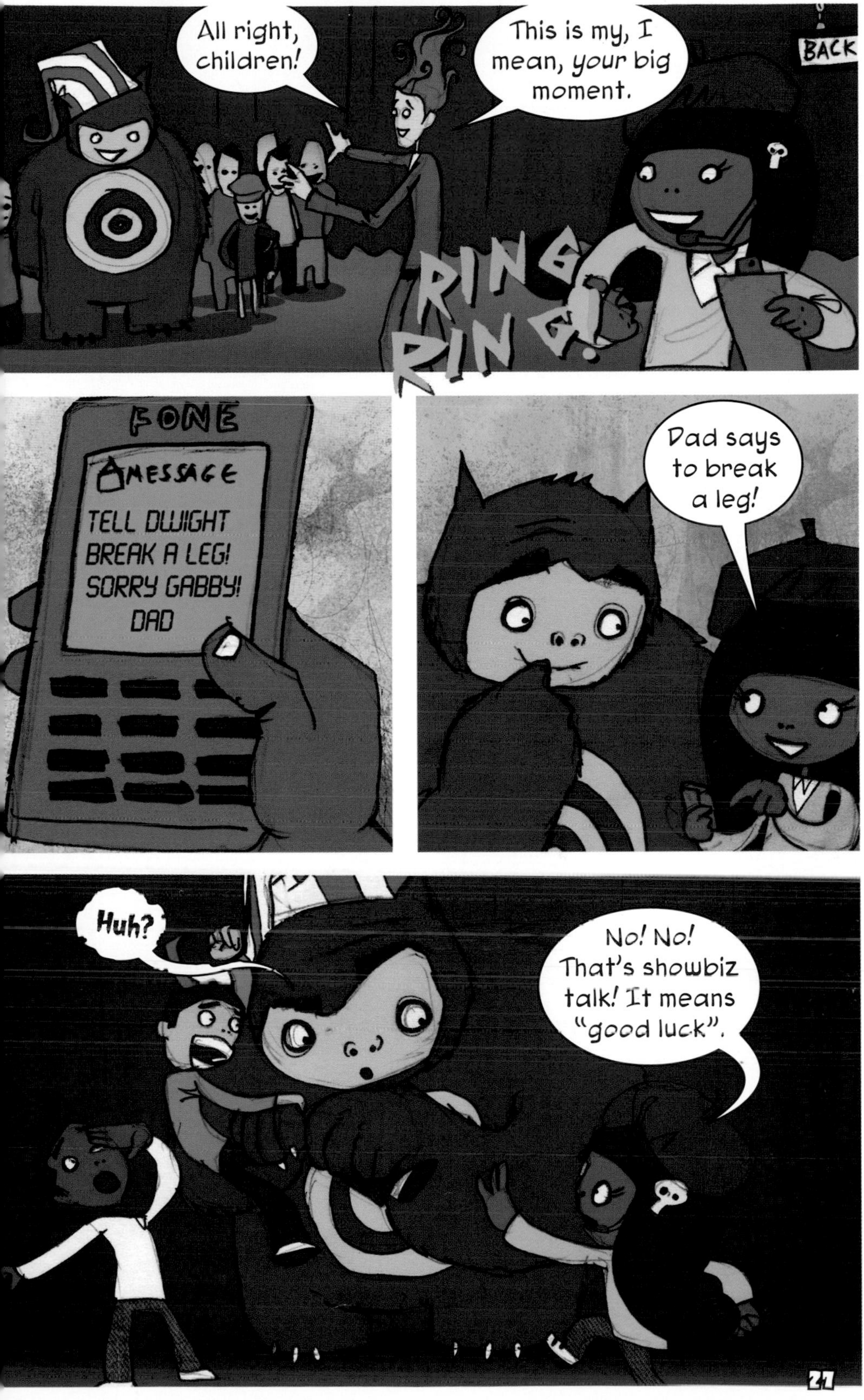
All right, children!
This is my, I mean, your big moment.
BACK
RING RING!
FONE
MESSAGE
TELL DWIGHT BREAK A LEG! SORRY GABBY! DAD
Dad says to break a leg!
Huh?
No! No! That's showbiz talk! It means "good luck".

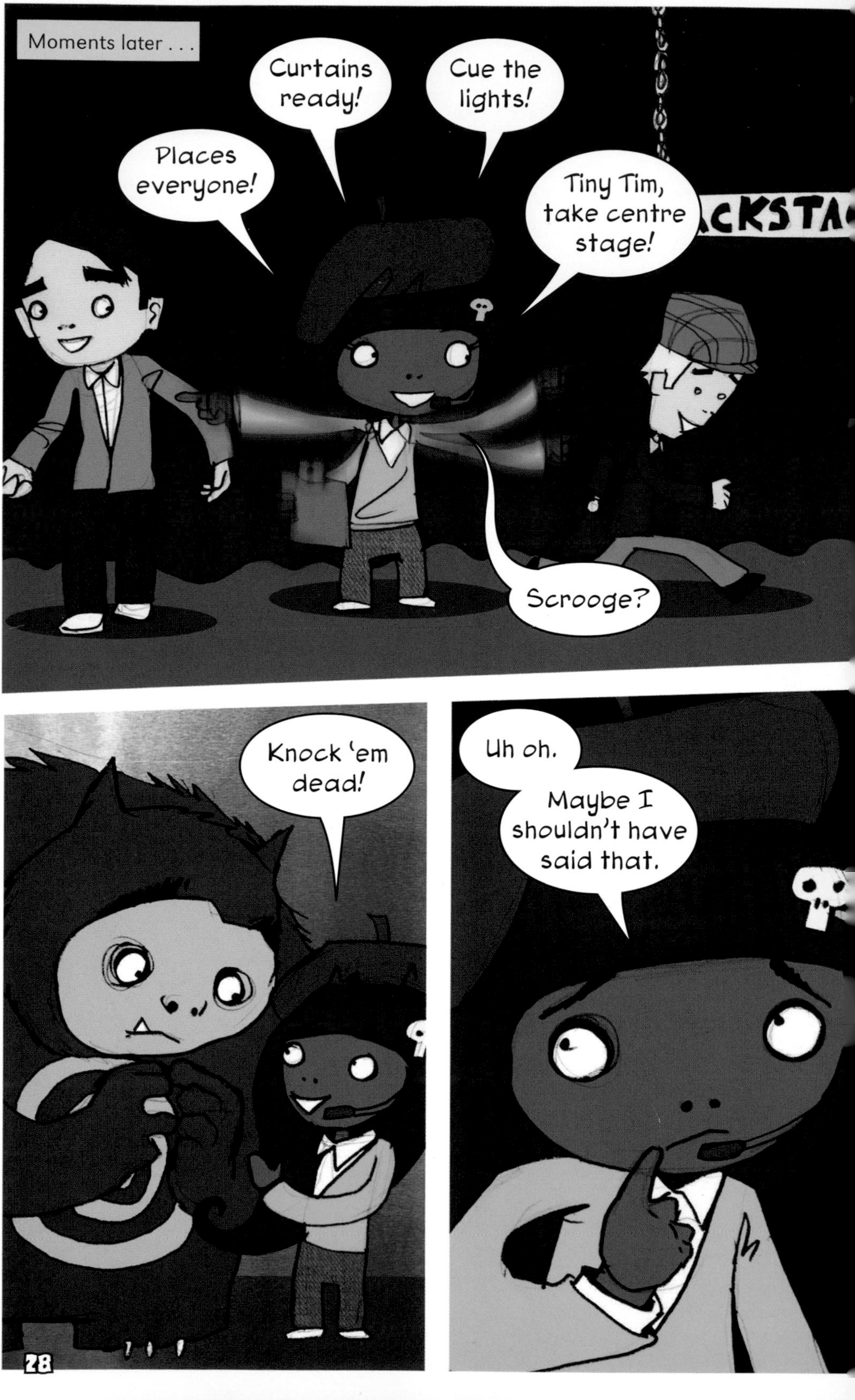
Moments later . . .
Places everyone!
Curtains ready!
Cue the lights!
Tiny Tim, take centre stage!
Scrooge?
Knock 'em dead!
Uh oh.
Maybe I shouldn't have said that.

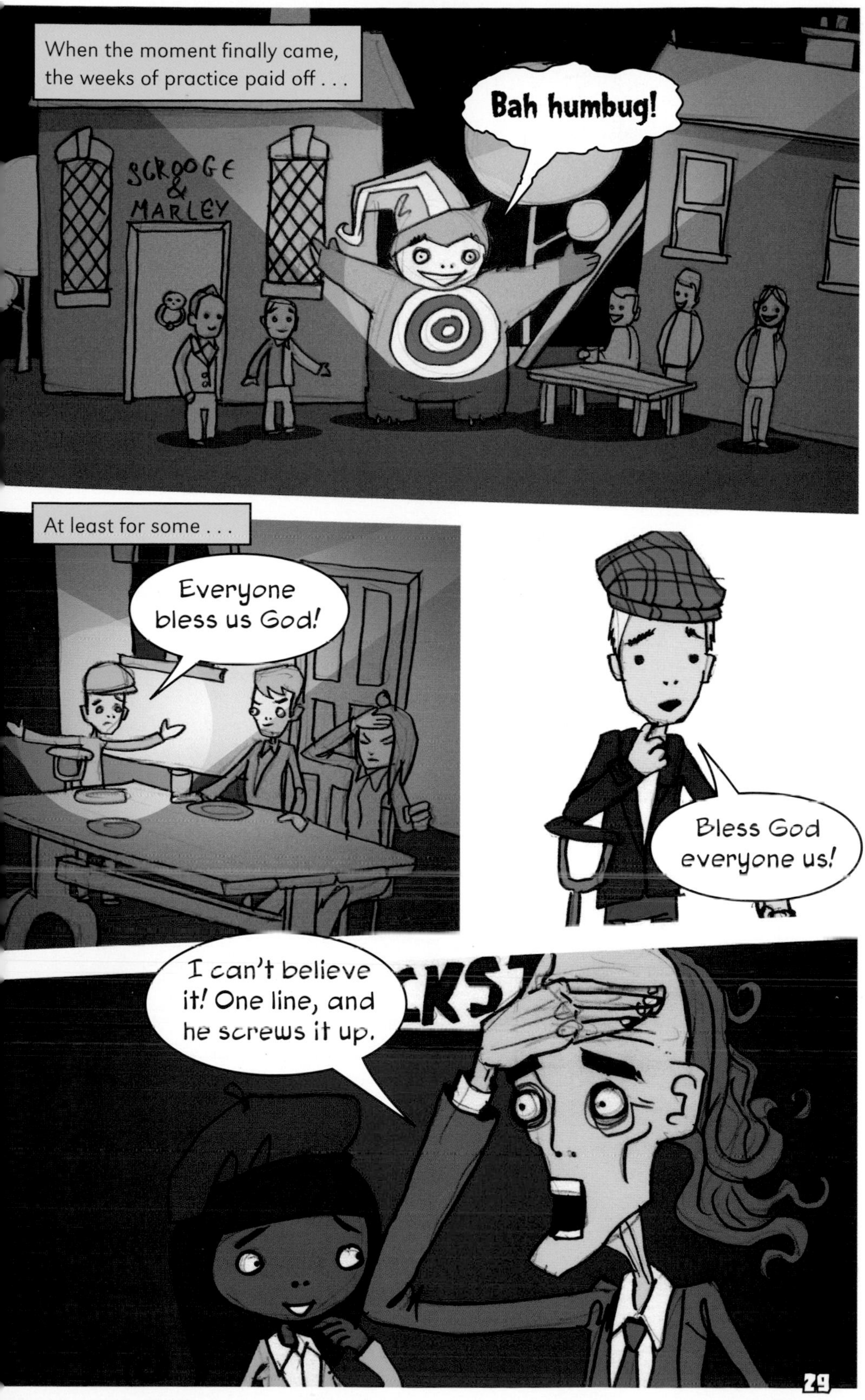
When the moment finally came, the weeks of practice paid off . . .
SCROOGE & MARLEY
Bah humbug!
At least for some . . .
Everyone bless us God!
Bless God everyone us!
I can't believe it! One line, and he screws it up.

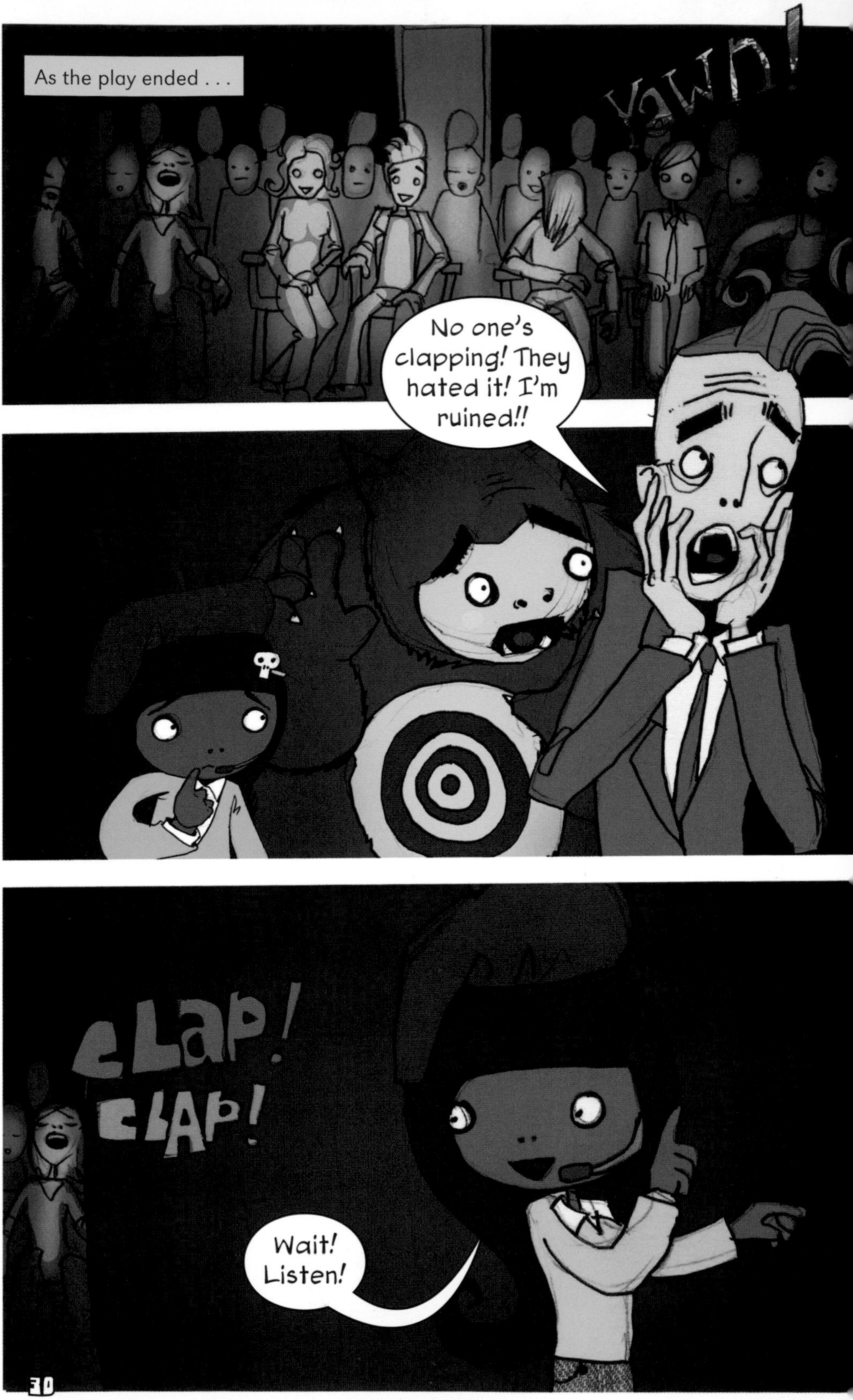
As the play ended . . .
Yawn!
No one's clapping! They hated it! I'm ruined!!
CLAP!
CLAP!
Wait! Listen!

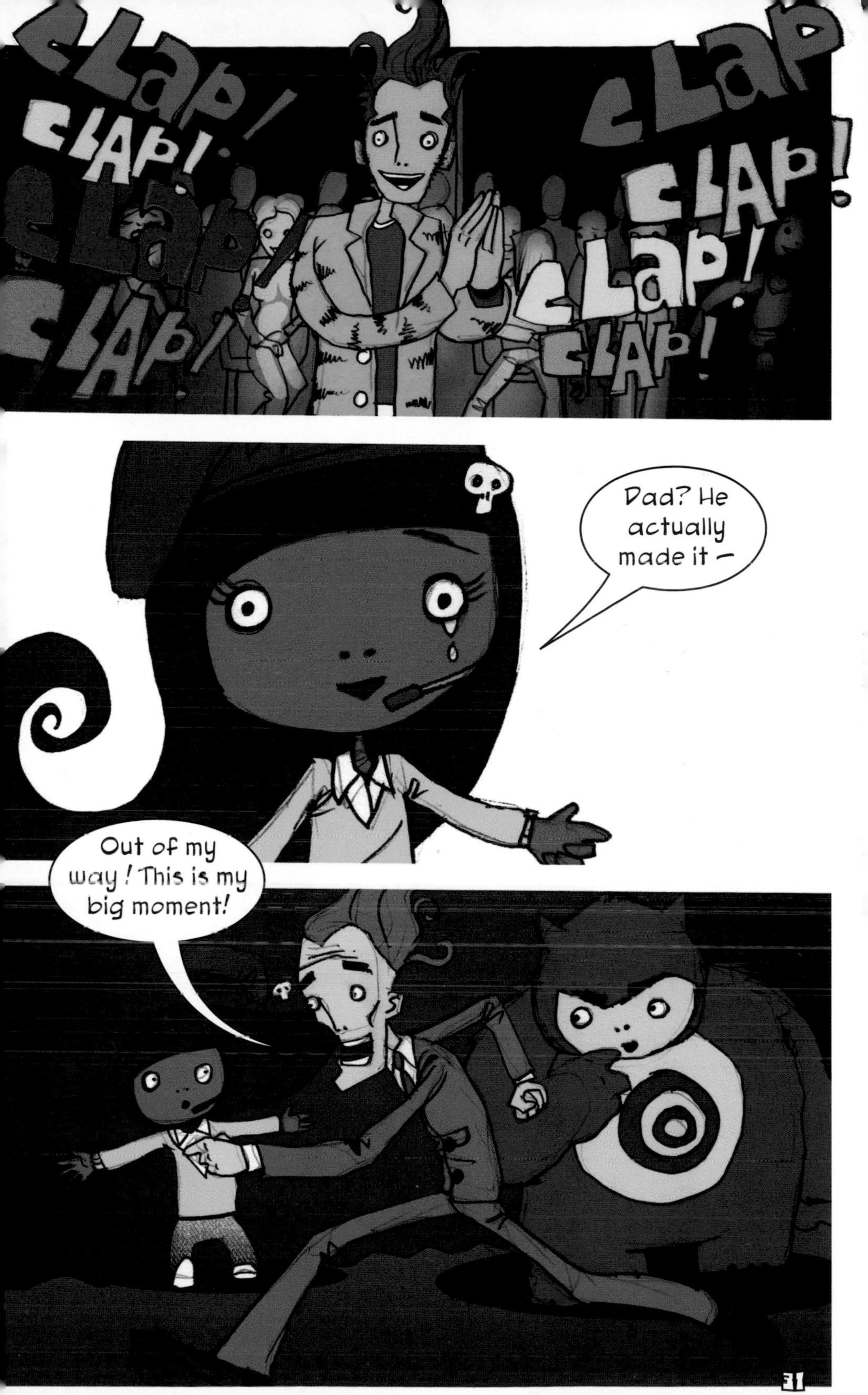
CLAP!
CLAP!
CLAP!
CLAP!
CLAP!
CLAP!
CLAP!
CLAP!
Dad? He actually made it –
Out of my way! This is my big moment!

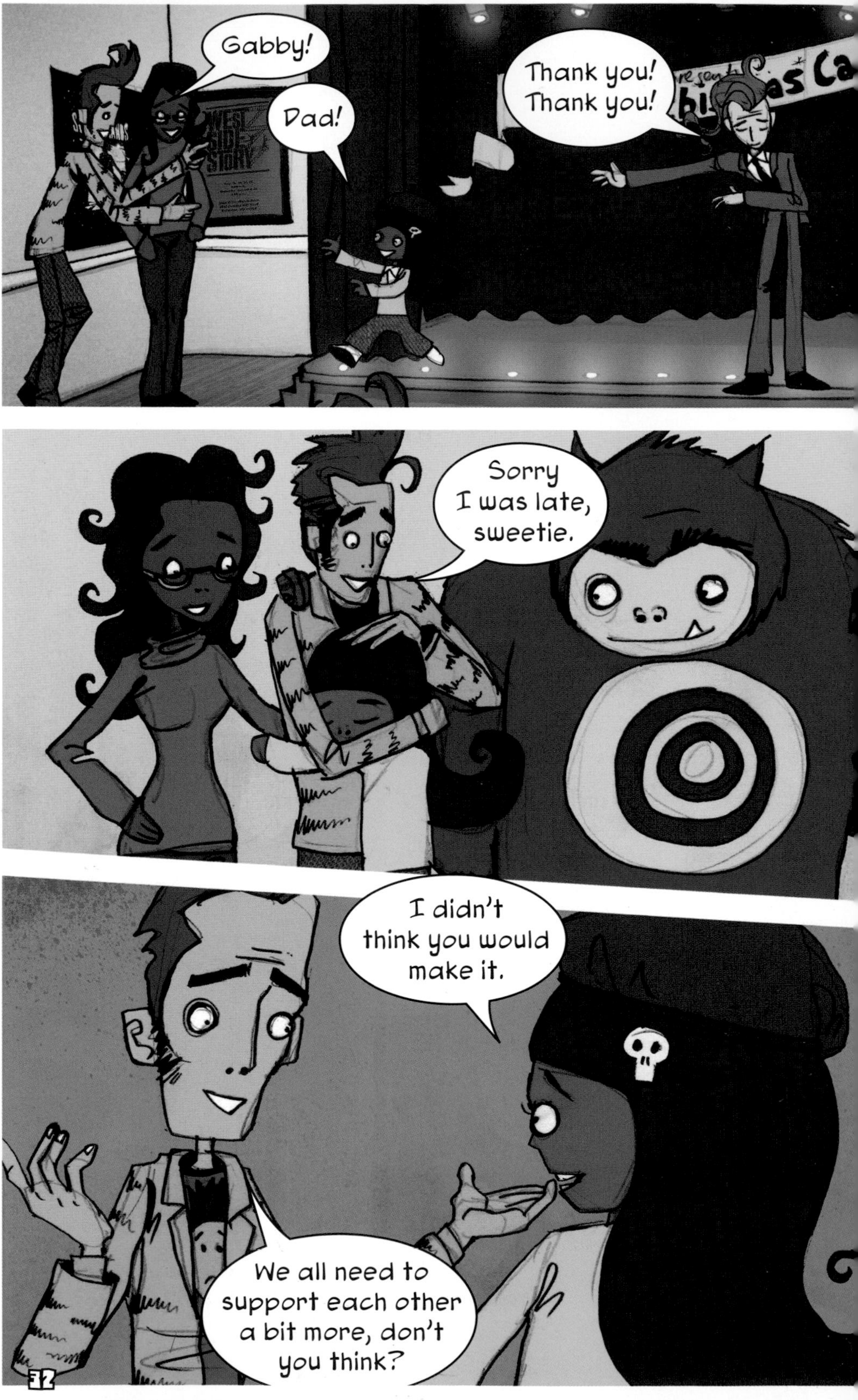
Gabby!
Dad!
Thank you! Thank you!
Sorry I was late, sweetie.
I didn't think you would make it.
We all need to support each other a bit more, don't you think?

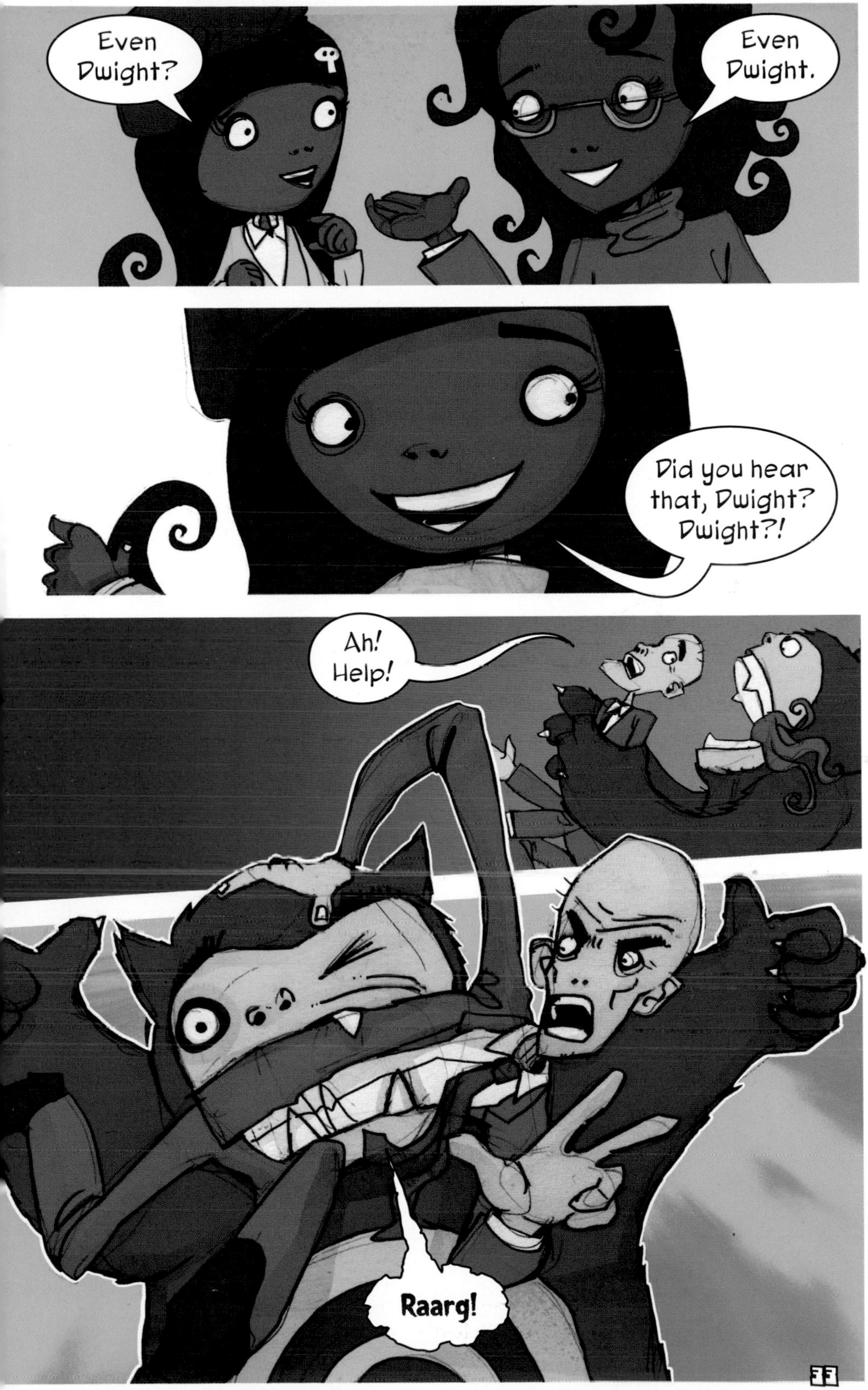
Even Dwight?
Even Dwight.
Did you hear that, Dwight? Dwight?!
Ah! Help!
Raarg!

HOW TO DRAW A MONSTER

YOU'LL NEED:

- a pencil
- a piece of paper
- a rubber (or two!)

1.

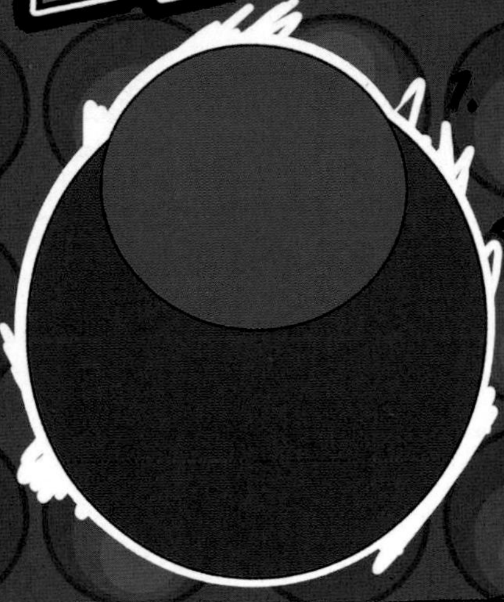

Monsters are often big and scary! Start by drawing a large oval for your monster's body. Then, draw a smaller circle on top of the body. This will become its head.

2.

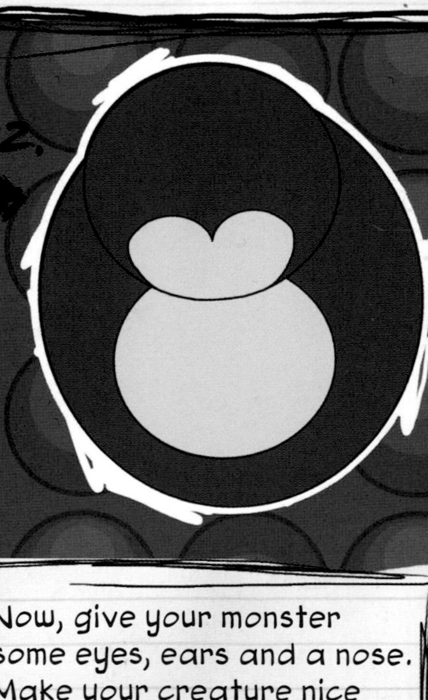

Draw another circle on the body. This will be your monster's tummy. For its face, add the top of a heart shape to your monster's head.

3.

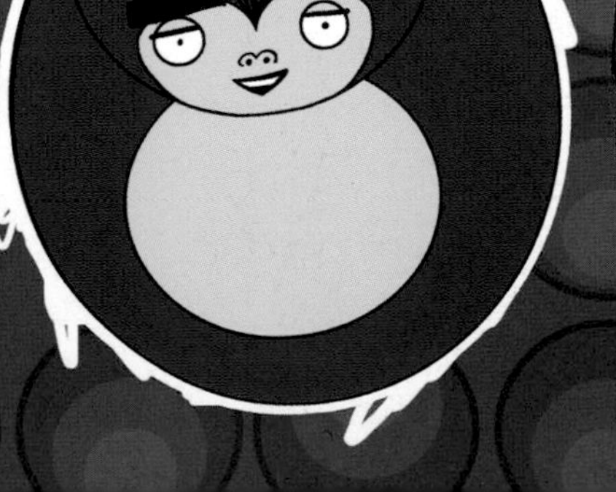

Now, give your monster some eyes, ears and a nose. Make your creature nice (like Dwight), or add some sharp fangs to make your monster really mean.

Next, draw your monster's arms and legs. Use the rubber to connect these parts to the body.

4.

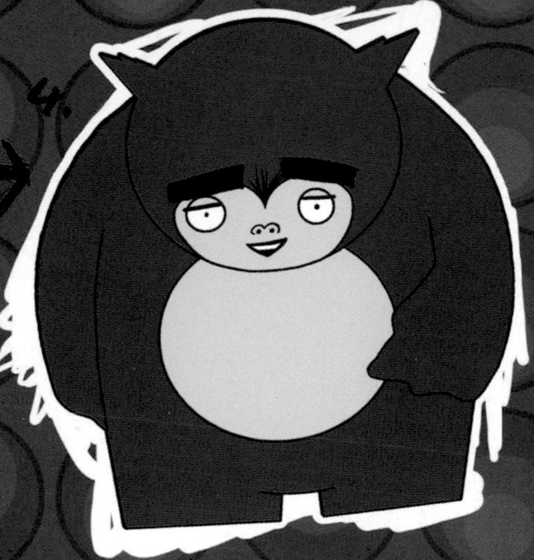

5.

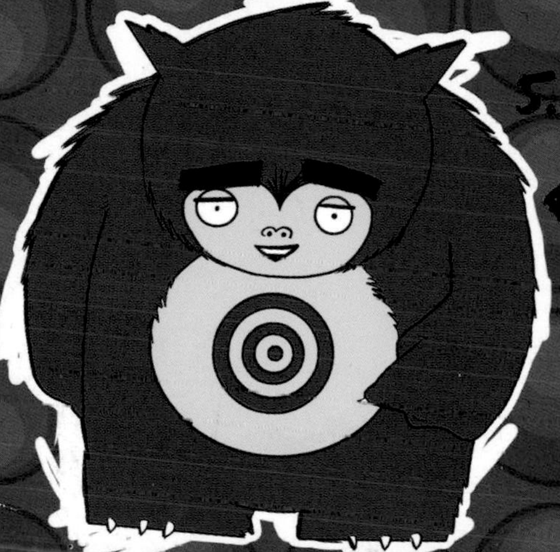

When your monster is almost finished, draw in the details. Maybe add a bull's-eye to its tummy, or give it some claws. It's up to you!

6.

Colour the monster in however you like, and then give your new creature a name. Make him a Purple People Eater, a Berry Blue Bogeyman or simply call him Dwight.

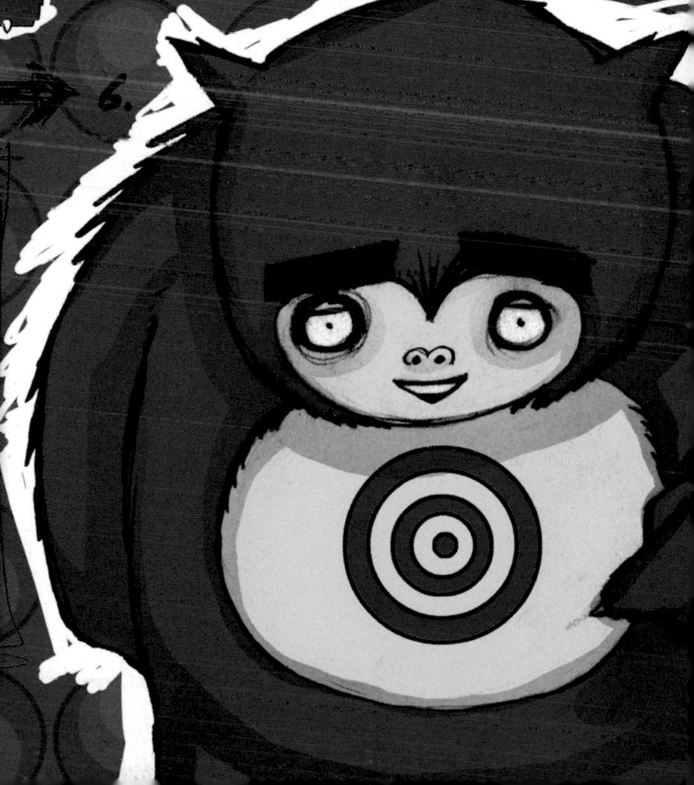

AUTHOR

Robert Marsh grew up in Omaha, Nebraska, USA, but longed to live somewhere else. He pretended not to live in Omaha by reading lots of books. Every week, Marsh checked out 20 books from the library. As he didn't have time to read all of those books, he would read the first chapter of each and make up the rest of the story. Marsh now makes up stories for a living and doesn't live in Omaha. Dreams do come true.

ILLUSTRATOR

Tom Percival grew up in Shropshire, a place of such remarkable beauty that he decided to sit in his room every day, drawing pictures and writing stories. But that was a long time ago, and much has changed since then. Now, Percival lives in Bristol, where he sits in his room all day, drawing pictures and writing stories. His patient girlfriend, Liz, and their baby son, Ethan, keep him company.

GLOSSARY

blubbering crying noisily

enrolled signed or joined up for a class, school or club of some kind

equal rights the right of all humans (and monsters) to be treated the same

ghoul an evil spirit, monster or ghost

growling making a deep, low, angry noise

humbug nonsense

ovation loud applause and cheering

self-esteem a feeling of personal pride or respect for yourself

showbiz short for the term "show business," which refers to the entertainment industry

whine to complain or moan in an annoying way

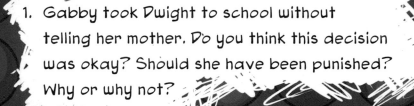
DISCUSSION QUESTIONS

1. Gabby took Dwight to school without telling her mother. Do you think this decision was okay? Should she have been punished? Why or why not?

2. Gabby and her monster, Dwight, are part of the school play. Have you ever participated in a play or other school activity? What was your favourite part of the experience?

3. At the end of the book, Dwight chomps down on the drama teacher, Mr Broadway. Do you think he'll be allowed back at the school? Why or why not?

WRITING PROMPTS

1. Imagine that you have a pet monster. What type of things would you do with it? Would your monster be scary or nice? Write about it.

2. Write another story about Gabby and her pet monster, Dwight. What will their next adventure be like? You decide.

3. Gabby and Dwight are part of their school play. Write a short play of your own. Who are the characters? What will they say and do? When you have finished, act out your play with the help of friends or family.

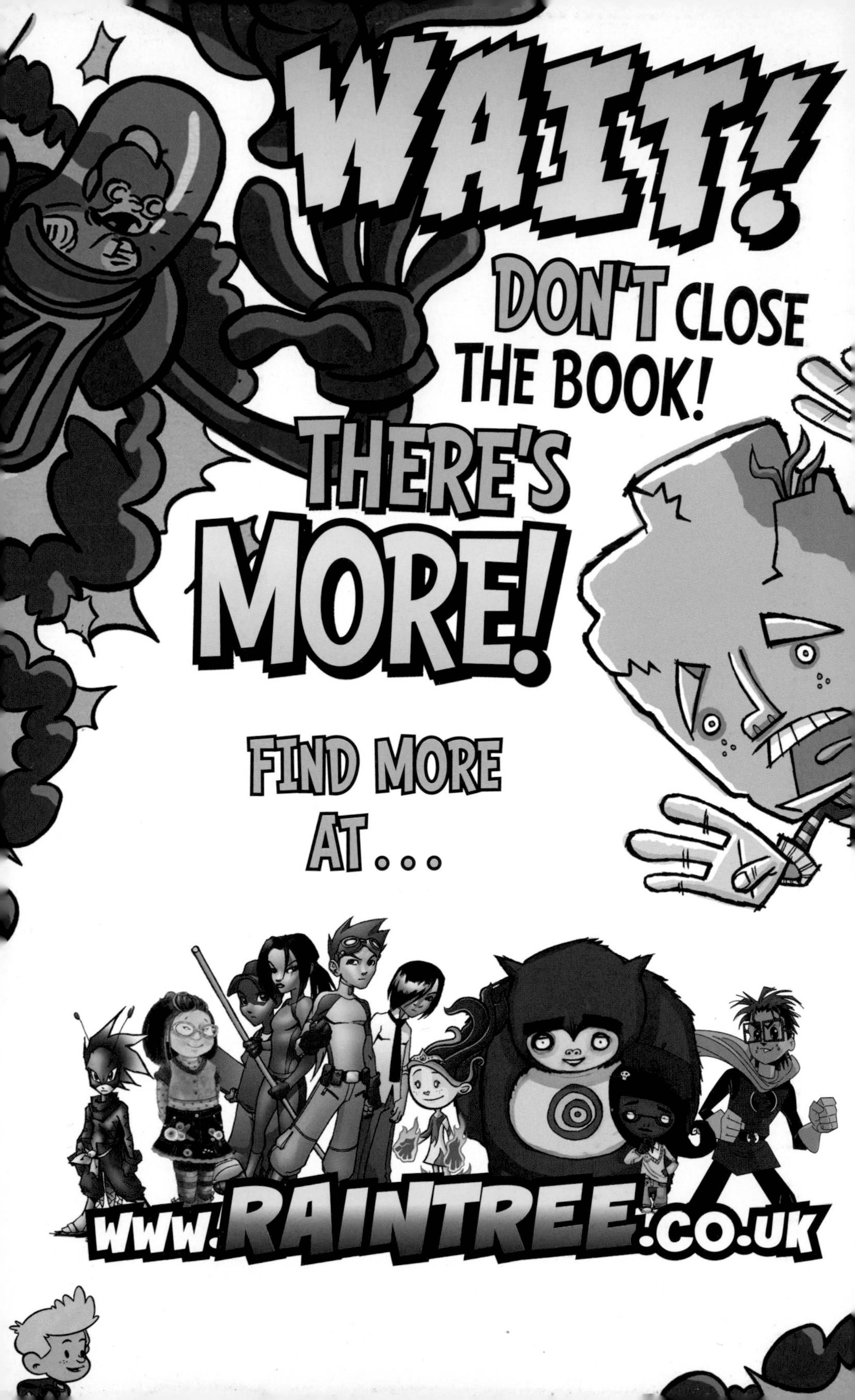
WAIT!
DON'T CLOSE THE BOOK!
THERE'S MORE!
FIND MORE AT...
WWW.RAINTREE.CO.UK